No Such Country

No Such Country

Gary Crew

19678

FiC
CRE

SIMON & SCHUSTER BOOKS FOR YOUNG READERS

Published by Simon & Schuster

New York London Toronto Sydney Tokyo Singapore

SIMON & SCHUSTER BOOKS FOR YOUNG READERS
1230 Avenue of the Americas, New York, New York 10020
Copyright © 1991 by Gary Crew
Originally published in Australia in 1991 by William Heinemann Australia, a
division of Reed International Books, Australia.
First U.S. edition 1994
Designed by David Neuhaus
The text for this book is set in Zapf Calligraphic
Manufactured in the United States of America

10 9 8 7 6 5 4 3 2 1

Library of Congress Cataloging-in-Publication Data
Crew, Gary No such country / by Gary Crew.   p.   cm.
Summary: When an anthropology student, hoping to learn about his Aborigi-
nal heritage, comes to work near their isolated village, sixteen-year-old friends
Sarah and Rachel discover why the man known as the Father has had such
control over their lives.   [1. Australia—Fiction. 2. Australian aborigines—
Fiction.]
I. Title. PZ7.C867No 1993 [Fic]—dc20 93-17619 CIP

ISBN: 0-671-79760-3

It is very certain, that the Discovery of Terra Australis Incognita is considered, by many wise and knowing People, as a kind of Philosopher's-stone, perpetual motion, or, in plain English, as a Chimera, fit only to take up the empty Brains of wild Projectors. Yet this seems to be no sufficient reason, why such as are competent Judges of the Matter in Dispute, should decide, peremptorily, that there is no such Country; or, if there be, that it is not worth the finding.

(A Complete Collection of Voyages and Travels, *John Campbell (Ed.), London, 1744–48)*

Dark night time, night time Bethliem
All sleep wake and get up
Mother likes him child christ clean white baby.

(R.M. Berndt, "Surviving Influences of Mission Contact on the Daly River, Northern Territory of Australia," 1952, cited in The White Men, *Julia Blackburn, Orbis Publishing Ltd, London, 1979.)*

Prologue

There were those who believed that the Father had existed from the beginning, that in some dark and primal time he had come up from the sea, flying like a white bird, or a vessel, some said, a white-sailed vessel, and that he had first appeared out of the surf at the entrance to the lagoon.

Now these possibilities could be true or could be superstition, but they were, nonetheless, used to account for the Father's remarkable dress, that he wore only white; by day he was most often seen walking the sandy paths of New Canaan in a suit of white cotton, black umbrella in hand; but by night, or in spiritual circumstances, he would make his appearance in a flowing cassock—likewise white—of the lightest, finest wool.

There were also those who believed that the Father kept a book, the great book, and in its pages he recorded the passing of their days. And not recorded only, some said, but created as he recorded, bringing their lives to be.

Truly, this white Father was a being of many parts: king and priest, friend and confessor [though some said monster and liar, but not often or out loud]. A creature of uncertain origins, uncertain intentions and designs.

Who could know his ways?

Signs and Wonders

I

One summer night there appeared in the sky over the lagoon at New Canaan a configuration of stars in the shape of an hourglass. This was the first of a series of strange occurrences which later became known as "signs." Of course, since this "apparition," as some called it, was not visible to all, there were few who paid the incident much attention at the time, and this included the Father, who was considered an authority on such things. But later "the sign of the hourglass," as it came to be called, was spoken of only in whispers, and with deep foreboding.

The circumstances of that first sighting were these: it was Saturday night in New Canaan; the local fishing fleet was in, and as usual, the sounds of men drinking came from the Fisherman's Rest. From a shed at the back of the store, opposite the Rest, two women appeared, dressed in the sensible manner that the Father approved and performing the duties that the Father had allotted. Between them they dragged a wooden cart, and emerging from the shadow of the store, they turned toward the moonlit path that led through the tea trees to the lagoon. A large cod had been taken in the nets that day, and since this needed to be smoked in preparation for the Father's table, the women were gathering wood from among the long-dead mangroves whose scattered limbs and clumps of silvered roots littered the shores of New Canaan.

At the end of the tea-tree path, they entered a sandy clearing, an isolated place and little visited. On one side lapped the lagoon, its waters wide and still; on the other was the lantana, an impenetrable thicket of fetid, fleshy leaves and rasping canes. This place was known as an Abode of Darkness, being so named by the Father, and shunned.

Nevertheless, the women showed no fear, and leaving the cart in the center of the clearing, they set about their task. First they worked together to lift and load the mangrove trunks, and later they separated, bending to gather the limbs half-buried in the sand, and having laid these across their arms in rigid sheaves, they dumped their harvest into the cart. When this had been done several times, one woman, Eva Burgess, pressed her hands against her back and arched forward, stretching, and as she glanced up, she saw an hourglass rising from the mist above the bar at the entrance to the lagoon. Immediately she called to her companion, Miriam Goodwin, and both women looked, filled with wonder.

The hourglass was formed entirely of stars. Some of these, which sparkled white and brilliant, showed the curves of its external shape, while others, which glowed rather than sparkled, appeared as its internal sands.

And as the glass moved, traveling in an arc across the heavens, peaking high over the lagoon and dropping low to vanish directly above the lantana, the sands fell. When first seen, the upper bowl was full, but when it disappeared, all had fallen to the lower bowl, leaving the upper void.

After the phenomenon had passed and they were left gaping at the empty heavens, the women realized the possibilities of what they had seen yet lacked the knowledge to interpret. Since their cart was not three-quarters full, they agreed that it would be best to complete their task quickly—and so satisfy the Father —then go to their husbands, in the hope that their experience of the sea and the night sky might offer an explanation of the event.

As the Father walked in his garden to take the night air and looked toward the Rest, there on the track before it, washed in the yellow light that spilled from its open door, he saw the women beckoning for their husbands to come out. Knowing this interruption of the men's drinking to be remarkable, he went down to learn the reason. He did not approach directly—

that was never his way, not from the beginning—but lingered in the shadows, observing and listening, and so he learned of the sighting.

When he had heard enough, he stepped out of the darkness into the light, his white robe suddenly bright with gold.

Smiling, he said, "Eva. Miriam. Ladies . . . Have you been at my wine?"

He meant the wine for the sacrament which he kept beneath his altar. Since they cleaned his church, the women knew.

"Father," Eva Burgess began, but he lifted his hands to signal silence.

When she stepped closer, attempting to speak again, he said, "Enough. Go home. We have no need of your troublesome ways."

The men snickered. Miriam touched her friend's arm and led her away.

But attitudes changed. Hardly a fortnight later the trawler *Seeker* went down and her crew drowned, under circumstances that stirred long-buried memories.

Aaron Steele, the owner of the *Seeker*, came from one of the original New Canaan families. His grandfather could remember when the Father had planted the twin cypresses which marked the entrance to the town, and from the beginning the Steeles had been successful fishermen, a circumstance directly attributed to their continued production of sons.

On the night before the tragedy, Steele and his sons,

Pete and Aaron junior, had trawled since sundown and taken nothing. At first light, as they were about to come in, they ran across a school of mullet and withdrew from the fleet to net alone. By midmorning, when the *Seeker* headed for the lagoon, she was loaded and sitting low in the water, and on that late tide she hit the bar and bottomed, her screw churning the sand. In minutes she had turned sideways to the outward run of the current while the surf pounded her in wave after wave.

No one could have seen this from the level of the lagoon jetties, not over the spray and surf at the bar, but the Father, who happened to be walking in the high dunes, looked down and raised the alarm, so that the town came out to watch.

From the dunes everyone could see Steele at the bridge, wrestling with the helm, and the boys on deck, upending crates of mullet, desperately trying to raise the stern to free themselves.

But it was too late. Aaron junior, who was only fourteen, grabbed at the nets which had been strung from the gantry and hung from them. His older brother, seeing his terror, went to him and spread his arms around him, cradling him in the web of the net, and their cries carried clear across the lagoon. Their father abandoned the helm and left the bridge, but no sooner had he appeared in the open than he was swept away and vanished, and at once the vessel leapt from the water to stand momentarily on its stern, then dropped back, rolling over and over, shattering as it rolled, and the boys were taken together.

In the morning Steele's body was found dumped on the ocean beach, but it was three days before the bodies of his sons appeared. Still entangled in their father's net, they drifted into the quiet water of the lagoon and washed up there, on the bank below the mangrove clearing. From the web of the net, their limbs sprawled, coated in black mud.

It was at this time that the first talk of "signs" began.

Then followed the fire at the core, an event witnessed by all New Canaan.

The core was a mountain of basalt, the cone-shaped plug of an ancient volcano, rising to a peak two hundred yards above the swamp to the north of town. Though it was solid rock—as the inhabitants of New Canaan knew well, having quarried it for building since the beginning—from every crack and fissure thorn apples sprouted, their barbs so sharp and dense that any attempt at ascent had been defeated.

Five days after the discovery of the bodies in the net, in that deeper darkness that comes before dawn, the core erupted in flames, as it had done, no doubt, millennia before. Within seconds the whole town was out, staring into the red glare of the sky. Then the air was gone, sucked up by flames, so the people in their nightwear clutched chests and throats, choking. And hardly had the air gone than the wind came pouring down the silent paths between the houses, rushing like a tide, and the witnesses, still grappling with the spectacle of the mountain and the sky and gasping in the airlessness, were struck suddenly and driven back against walls and fences, suffocating and amazed.

Then came a rain of ashes. For three days this fell, and houses, boats, jetties, the church itself—all of New Canaan—was shrouded in gray, leveling and morbid. It was not only the settling ash which caused distress; occasionally a glowing sprig of thorns would drift gently down to smolder in the stiffened folds of a wind-dried wash or burst into orange flame among the heaps of withered leaves, tinder dry, that clogged the shallow gutters of every building in the town.

And after the ashes came the storms. Above the horizon, lightning quivered in sheets of vivid flame, the wind lashed at the bar, and the waves were mountainous and heavy with kelp.

One morning, after a night of particular violence, Eva Burgess and Miriam Goodwin were at their places on the jetty, picking rubbish from their husbands' nets and talking softly, as was their way, when Eva stopped and said, "Ouch," then put the index finger of her right hand into her mouth and sucked it.

"Something sharp," she said, and within seconds she was squeezing the thumb of her left hand against the veins of her right wrist and looking in terror into the face of her friend.

"I've been stung," she said, "or bitten," and she fell forward onto the planks, her breath coming in short, agonized gasps, her limbs contorted.

And so she died, her head thrown back against Miriam's chest, her shoulders gripped in Miriam's arms, and her thin cotton skirt spilled wide about both as a pool of ruby-red blood.

Yet, since neither woman had cried out nor made any fuss, it was not until much later that the men realized something was wrong and found them locked together.

When the net was lifted, there on the planks was a seasnake, coiled among the matted weed, its silver scales banded in shining jet; it seemed comfortable, or satisfied, its milky eyes and gummy mouth belying the potency of its venom.

And then, in the dim and smoky recesses of the Fisherman's Rest, or over tea and caraway cake, bitter and sliced thin, the word went around to "watch out," to read "the signs," but as no one knew what to watch for, or when or where, this vigilance became a strange and solitary thing, carried out chiefly at night, in staring wide-eyed at pale and drifting curtains or wondering at the soft, slow lapping of the sea.

None was so unsettled as the Father, and although he told his flock that such signs were indeed wondrous doings and that the net of the evil one should terrify only the wicked and the guilty, he observed all, missing nothing, and was said to have recorded every incident, every detail of every sign, in the pages of his great book.

Annunciation

I

The cemetery at New Canaan was not part of the town. It lay beyond the limits of the twin cypresses, some distance along the swamp road in the shadow of the core. Decades before, an attempt had been made to fence the place, but two basalt plinths, cut from the core quarry and no doubt intended to support entry gates, were all that remained of this enterprise.

In the event of a funeral—a circumstance common in New Canaan—there was no service at the church. The locals walked directly to the cemetery. Some took the swamp road, entering through the unfinished gate; others took the tea-tree path, and having followed it to the mangrove clearing, they skirted the lantana thicket to come upon the first of the gray and weathered headstones from the seaward side. While those who followed this path had always been few, no one chose to do so the day Eva Burgess was buried.

Beside the open grave the mourners waited in silence for the arrival of the coffin, a casket of undressed pine, rough, and teetering awkwardly on the shoulders of the fishermen. After this came the Father, his white robes stark in the dazzling noon. When he had taken his place at the edge of the pit and seen the coffin partially lowered, he threw back his head and, casting his gray eyes to the heavens, delivered the office of the dead, concluding by raising his arms and crying, "Watch the signs, people of New Canaan. Watch the signs. For surely the evil one comes, roaming even the sunlit paths, to gather all in his net of souls. Therefore be ready and watching, and so live that none are taken unprepared, for tomorrow is a day uncertain, and you know not when, nor where, the net shall be cast. . . . " In response the people murmured:

> *"Father, guide us,*
> *Guide us in the paths;*
> *Father, guide us,*
> *Guide us all our lives."*

And he raised his arms higher, as if to bless.

Yet some remained silent. Opposite the Father stood Miriam Goodwin, mute since her friend's death; and beside her were two girls: her daughter, Sarah, and Rachel Burgess, the daughter of Eva. Neither had joined in the response to the Father. At fifteen, with an open grave yawning before them, the girls were wise enough to recognize change when they saw it.

Rachel and Sarah had been born only hours apart, to the delight of their mothers, and since any birth had become the exception in New Canaan, this peculiar circumstance attracted considerable attention. The Father selected their names, and their mothers did not argue, having learned very early to respect his will.

But over the years, in the opinion of the locals, the girls proved a disappointment.

Rachel grew trim and agile, delighting in movement —always wanting to do something, to go somewhere —and when this energy was matched with the seaside tawniness of her skin and her sleek dark hair, which she kept cut short, she appeared born to work on the jetties. Some had told Eva that her daughter was almost the equal of a son, but those who said so had reckoned without the surety of intelligence that flashed and challenged from Rachel's deepbrown eyes and she was soon considered "too spirited for a female" and "in need of management," opinions endorsed by the Father, who regarded her as dangerous.

Sarah was the younger of the two—a circumstance Rachel would never allow her to forget—and she could not have been more different. Sarah was fairskinned, freckled, big and clumsy. Never an outdoors girl, she was happy to sit, talking or dreaming, twisting her long coppery hair, or reading, although in New Canaan she found little to satisfy her. "A big girl with a lot of brains," her mother would say, not intending to hurt. But Sarah soon recognized her physical inadequacies, adjusting to them as a matter of little choice rather than accepting them, and her size did not concern her; she knew her own mind. This common sense, along with her reading, was what she most valued, apart from the respect of her mother and, of course, Rachel.

With these qualities and the close and exclusive nature of their friendship, it was hardly surprising that in a small town such as New Canaan—among small-town minds with small-town attitudes—neither of the girls was liked, and as they grew, if the locals thought of them at all, it was in terms of seeing them "married off early," an arrangement the Father strongly advocated.

But their mothers wanted better for the girls. They organized the Fish Board pickup to collect Rachel and Sarah every morning, dropping them at school in the city, and every afternoon, at five, they came home to New Canaan with the deliveries for the store, sitting on upturned crates, bouncing along the swamp road in the back of a van, smelling of fish, tarred rope, or fuel, or whatever else was on board at the time. And always Sarah would read, either from road signs or labels on cartons or magazines or sodden newspapers splattered all over with fish scales, bloodied crimson, "like sequins," she would say, and together they would giggle and laugh, filled with delight at the mar-

velous possibilities of their future, never once doubt-
ing that they would go somewhere, be somebody.

But when Eva Burgess died and Miriam Goodwin
withdrew into silence, the girls were allotted their
mothers' duties and their education ceased.

Now, as the coffin came to rest, and the sand was
shoveled in to cover it, Rachel wept for the mother
she had lost and the end of her dreams.

Seeing her in tears, Sarah whispered, "I'm here. You
have to remember that I'm here."

Rachel nodded, ashamed of her thoughts, but as
she lifted her head, the eyes of the Angel Rossellini
met hers across the grave, and the realization of her
long-term future came to her at once.

II

Angelo Rossellini, known to the locals as the Angel,
had not appeared at a funeral before, and for this
first time, he had turned out in style. He wore a blue
double-breasted suit belonging to his father, with a
white shirt and a tie, also blue, and when Rachel
looked again, she saw him struggling to undo the col-
lar button beneath. But in spite of his obvious discom-
fort, he looked good, square shouldered like a man,
though he was only seventeen, little more than a year
older than the girls.

The Angel was respected in New Canaan—even

revered—although he would never go to sea. No one could talk about the reason for this with any certainty, but there was a story that when he was a child of seven, his father had taken him out one night, just the two of them, and something came up beside the boat. Monstrous things from the deep surfaced from time to time if a boat was working well out and if the night was very dark with no moon. There would be a heave from beneath the keel and the boat would lift from the water and sit there, as if on air, then a second later ease back, and with a ripple and a terrible long sigh, whatever it was would be gone, back down into the awful darkness it had come from.

They say that this happened to the Angel; that he was working on the deck of his father's boat when one of those things came up for a visit, but all that anybody ever knew for certain about the episode was that they saw Papa Rossellini come in that morning and half-carry, half-drag his pale and quivering son up the track from the lagoon to the Fisherman's Rest, where he set him on the bar and poured brandy into him, and all the while the boy whimpered, "The eyes, Papa, I seen the eyes."

After that, although the Angel would work on the jetties, he would never go to sea. Locals said that it was this fear that led him to spend his free time— even as a boy—working in the Father's garden at the church, but whatever the reason, the Angel developed a peculiar bond with the Father, and this relationship, coupled with his good looks and powerful build, caused people to be wary of him and to defer to his wishes. All, that is, except for Rachel Burgess.

III

Three or four days after the funeral, when the girls sat on the jetty as their mothers had done, sorting the catch, Sarah said, "The Angel could change. He could mature and grow into something decent. Besides, you could never say he was ugly. He's got black hair and blue eyes, which is something, and a good face, and a square jaw, like those models in magazines, and his mouth is what they call sensual. . . ."

Rachel looked at her. "Sarah," she said, "are we talking about someone for me or for you? I mean, does the Angel appeal to you, or what?"

Sarah laughed. "You know who he's after, and has been since the beginning. You know as well as I do why he went to your mother's funeral and stood where he did, right opposite you. So don't put on that dumb act with me."

"But I don't want him," Rachel said. "And I never have. Sure, I can see that he would scrub up physically, but . . ."

"Physically?" Sarah snorted. "Physically? You think that either of us could expect to find any more than a decent body in this place? Now that the Steele boys

are gone, we would be hard up even finding a male—
one who is less than fifty, that is. So maybe you should
have a go with the Angel. Work on him. Clean him
up. I reckon you could . . . and he would do anything
for you."

Rachel wiped her hands on the cloth she kept
across her knees and looked Sarah in the eye. "OK,"
she said, "I'll do that. I'll go up to the depot and see
him. But only on the condition that while I'm making
out in the tea-tree scrub, or wherever he takes me . . ."

"To the Father's garden."

"OK. While I'm making out in the Father's garden,
you sit here and don't leave or attempt to follow me
or, worse still, to watch, until every one of the fish in
this crate has been sorted. And gutted . . ."

"And packed in ice?"

"And packed in ice. And stacked in the truck. Is that
a deal?"

They laughed then and were silent. But in reality it
was not so easy to laugh the Angel off.

IV

Like so many of the houses in New Canaan, the
Burgess place was a weatherboard bungalow, once
painted brown, with a low-pitched galvanized roof,
and verandahs back and front, intended to catch the

breeze. But since these verandahs were enclosed with screens of wire mesh to keep out insects, and the wire was corroded and encrusted with salt, the houses appeared sullen and brooding. There were no gardens, and the straggling scrub that crept up the paths and easements between the houses did nothing to relieve this mood. At night, particularly if there was no moon, New Canaan was a dismal place.

Since Rachel's father was a fisherman who went to sea at four each afternoon and did not come in until sunup, she spent her nights alone, and the Angel knew it.

He began to come around late, after ten, as she was preparing for bed. At first there were vague sounds like the scratchings of a bird on the tin roof, or an animal digging in the sandy yard, but then came the soft crunching of footsteps on dry grass and the hint of someone breathing. When the night was like this, and threatening, Rachel would sit quietly on the verandah, hardly moving except to breathe, looking out into the dark yard. Once or twice she had called out "Sarah?" all the while knowing that it was not, that it wouldn't be, and then, in a voice that she hoped would not betray her fear, "Angel? Is that you?"

He did not answer, but she was certain it was him. And the verandah light made matters worse; by the dim glow of its single bulb, he could see her through the enclosing screens, framed against the house. But the reverse did not apply. Beyond the lowest step, where the arc of light ended in a sharp line, the yard was black as pitch. So she learned to do without light, practicing simple jobs in darkness, or sitting by the hour in a rocking chair, quite still, her legs drawn up, her chin resting on her knees.

Then one night, when the wind had come up from the sea and the screens of the verandah warped and twisted, she got up, pushed open the screen door, and called into the darkness, "I know that you're there. Come out now. Right now. Or go away for good."

From the shadows beside the verandah, almost at her feet, he suddenly appeared, his head down, looking as uncomfortable as he had done at the funeral. In a way Rachel was relieved—at least it *was* only him. Still, she would not let on.

"Listen," she said, "you can't do this. You can't come hanging around here. I don't like it. I don't want you here."

He stood on the bottom step, hardly a yard from her. "Why not?" he said, his sheepishness gone. "There sure as hell isn't anybody else I'm going to be disturbing here, is there?"

It was a cruel remark, a direct reference to the death of her mother, but true enough, as Rachel knew— though she was not going to let it pass.

"Yes," she said. "You're right. There's nobody else. And if anybody knows, it's you. You've been snooping around since Mum died. I know it's you at night. Just stop it."

He came closer then, up to the top step, and looked down on her. She could smell the sweat beneath his thick shirt.

"I want to come here," he said, "to be near you. You've got no one. What's wrong with a man wanting to be near you? It's natural, isn't it? When a girl looks like you?"

He drew his left hand from his pocket and with his fingers stroked the hair fallen across her forehead. He had never spoken to her like this before, or touched her in this way. It was not rough, but she was suddenly afraid.

"Get," she said and caught his wrist to push him away. "Get. Get out!"

He laughed outright. "See? You say 'get' and then hold me. I'll get. But I'll come back too, because that's what you want. I know it."

Then he was gone, through the side gate into the dark lane beyond.

V

Nor was Rachel the only one whose nights were long; these were bad times for Sarah too—since the death of Eva Burgess, her mother had not spoken a word, and within a week of the funeral, it was apparent that Miriam Goodwin had surrendered all contact with reality. She ate, drank, and attended to her personal hygiene, but apart from these rituals of living, she denied any human intercourse and might as well have been dead herself. She had not attempted to continue her work at the jetty or attend to the Father's duties at the church, and though he called often, spoke to her in whispers, took her hand and stroked it, she would not respond but sat all day in a chair of woven cane, her head turned from the sea, staring out at the bush through the screens on the back verandah, as if seeking access to some other place, some other country, which lay in the shadow of the towering core.

What made life harder for Sarah, apart from caring for this new and peculiar person, was the added responsibility of an older brother, Joseph, a fisherman like his father. Unlike Rachel, who had only her father to keep house for, Sarah had to get up and do the breakfasts for both men, then sort the catch at the jetty, then wash, then get the house in order, and after that make the midday meal which they ate before leaving and the hot dinners they took with them every night.

And when they were not at sea, every Saturday night and Sunday, or during bad weather, they would go straight to the Fisherman's Rest, stock up on cheap rum—which they called Fisherman's Blood—then come home and proceed to drink themselves into a stupor. But before they lapsed into this state, there was always an argument about who had hauled the best catch that week or some other no-win contest they created for themselves, until a fight broke out.

So, being suddenly faced with new and fearful responsibilities, and knowing well the limited possibilities of escape, the girls set about the management of their separate households with a degree of acceptance, although inwardly each wrestled with her own misfortune, too afraid to heap more hurt on the other.

They met each morning on the jetty and talked about what they had cooked or how they had cleaned or what they had heard on the radio, or read, and any other bits and pieces of news that made up their days. But by the end of a month, there was not a great deal left to say, at least nothing of importance, and their lives wavered on the brink of the meaningless.

Then one afternoon, having seen her father and brother put to sea, Sarah decided it was time to make a change.

The weather was miserable, with showers driving in from the sea, and she pulled a chair up opposite her mother and said, "Well, Mum, I'm going to read something to you."

She produced a Bible which she kept in her room

and began to read aloud from the Twenty-third Psalm. Having read the part about the valley of the shadow of death and fearing no evil, she looked up and said, "Mum, are you listening to this?"

There was no hint of response. "Is all this a waste of time?" she asked.

Still no answer. Her mother stared steadily inland, through the haze of fly screen at the dank and dripping bush.

"Well," Sarah said, "I don't know what the Father says when he comes around and I don't care much, but I'm going to say something anyway. Because I can't make things any worse."

She closed the Bible and put it on the floor beside her, then, looking away from her mother toward the yard, said, "I think that what you're doing is wrong. At least as far as I'm concerned. It's not fair. I'm not even sixteen yet, but what you're doing is making me act like I'm fifty. I can see what it's all about, and in some ways I can't even blame you, now that I understand better about running this house. When I was going to school, I never even saw Dad or Joseph, I never had to worry about them. Not from your point of view, like the wife or the mother. Or like a housekeeper. Which is what you were, and I am now. I can understand all that, and I'm sorry about it, but it's me I want to know about—why I'm not good enough for you to live for, or even care about. Why is it that because your friend died, you have to give up living too? Only it's worse than that. She's dead, but you're only pretending. If you really wanted to be with her, you would do something about it—starve yourself or something—but you eat, and that says to me that you don't want to die. And why should you? What other woman in this place has two children? Check in the cemetery some time—you could think yourself lucky. So, if you can't be bothered living for Dad or Joseph but don't really want to die, well, try living for me, because I'm your daughter . . . and I love you."

She stood up and said, "I'm going to Rachel's. I'll try to be back by nine to make you a cuppa. And I know you heard every word that I said."

Then she opened the screen door and was gone.

Through the maze of weathered fences, sagging gates, and dismal bush, she made her way to Rachel's house. Though she heard the first sigh of the night wind and felt its chill against her face, she was not concerned. In no time at all she would be standing outside her friend's screen door calling, "Rachel, Rachel," as she had a thousand times before.

"And besides," she said to herself, "even if there was a net of souls, what evil one in its right mind would come looking to catch someone in this miserable place?"

Visitations

The locals heard the bike long before they saw it. This was midmorning on a Saturday, and the men had already gone up to the Fisherman's Rest, but when they heard the sound of the engine, even though it was way off along the swamp road, well outside of town, they took their beers and stood beside the track to wait and see; there was never much to look at in New Canaan.

While it is true that some went inside, supposing that the rider must have been lost in the first place and turned around—since the sound soon faded and died—those who remained saw a shape silhouetted in the tunnel of light between the cypresses; then came a glint of silver and the shape took form and became a man wheeling a motorbike, and as they watched, he stepped out of the shadows into the town.

At first he was too far away to be seen clearly, but as he came closer, all the while looking around him, they had their chance. He was about seventeen, easy in his movements, sure of himself. From his jeans, T-shirt, and jacket they could tell he was a city boy—not a man, as the locals knew men; he was everything they despised.

When he reached the Rest, where they stood gawking, he nodded and said, "The lagoon. Is there a place called the lagoon near here? Or a place that used to be called that?"

There was an uneasy shuffle, and someone pointed around the corner toward the tea-tree path, but not a word was spoken, so he walked on.

As he passed, they saw his canvas backpack and noticed the small pick suspended in a stirrup to one side, its metal head brand new and gleaming. Glances were exchanged, shoulders shrugged, sand kicked; then the locals took their beers and went in and the track before the Rest was clear, as it had been five minutes before.

Not everyone turned away and made no sound or move to follow. Rachel and Sarah were outside the store when the figure had stepped into the light and walked by where they stood.

Sarah said under her breath, "Rachel, look." But her friend had missed nothing. When the boy turned the corner and was out of sight, it was Rachel who ran in front of the church where he had turned, and stared after him.

Nor did she stop staring and go back to Sarah until she heard a sharp, dry cough behind her and saw a flash of white as the door of the church slammed shut.

Later this episode also became known as a sign; the sign of the one who walked in.

II

There was no breeze, not a breath. The lagoon lay sullen and brassy with sun. It was very hot.

No one would have seen Rachel slip away down the tea-tree path, leaving the drowsy afternoon house to her sleeping father. She walked lightly, her feet bare, and although the sand on the sunny patches was burning, she was not worried. She could leave the path altogether if she wanted. If she saw the Father down that way, she could simply step to one side. In her white shirt and shorts, she would be gone, absorbed in the mottled light between the trees.

There was no part of the lagoon that Rachel did not know—its treacherous bar, its reedy banks, its jetties and neglected sheds. Certainly she could sit with Sarah in the sun and sort the catch, or go farther and nestle herself high in the sandhills overlooking the sea, but of all these places the tea-tree path was her favorite. Here she would wander for hours, taking in everything about her.

The tea trees grew in clumps, the trunks no more than inches apart, and between them, springing from the sand, were soft grasses, very green, and patches of purple-berried ground cover or beds of fallen leaves, thick and cushioning. At times Rachel would drop down, bringing her knees up under her chin and wrapping her arms about, to watch the green ants move silently over the leaves or across her feet. She did not stir and was never bitten. At other times she would stop and, with a finger and thumb, strip the white tea-tree bark, thick and papery, then shred it to expose its layers, the pink, gray, and cream beneath the white; but she could not understand why, no matter how much bark was stripped, she never seemed to reach the trunk, the raw surface of the timber itself.

There were banksia groves too. Only a few, each of six or eight trees. Their trunks were gnarled, their branches twisted and bent low and massed with the hard brown brushes and cones of spent flowers. These were the trees that she climbed—"stepped up into," Sarah said, which was probably more honest since the branches arched down almost to the sand—but Rachel was still high enough to be hidden among the leaves and feel safe. In high summer, when the trees were in flower, the honey eaters would come hovering in front of her face, either ignorant of her presence or taking her limbs for branches and her hair for shadow.

This afternoon she was more than usually careful, very quiet in her movements. She knew the outsider was here somewhere. From in front of the church, she had watched him until he disappeared, and guessed that he had found the path and gone through to the lagoon; unless he had followed it only for a short distance, then cut through to the sandhills and the sea—or gone on to the end, to the lantana.

I'll find him, she thought. *And see him properly, just once. Then I will be satisfied, and tell Sarah.*

To her right she passed the jetties, but since this was Saturday, the one day of the week when no fishermen went out, they lay quiet and deserted, the boats moored, the great nets strung wide. After the jetties were the sheds and slipways where, once a year, each boat would be hauled for scraping and painting. But with the bar silting up and catches getting smaller and unknown reefs far out and cyclones and fire at sea, over the years the fleet had diminished, and on the gray and splintered timbers of the sheds, pale and fading, were the names of the lost: the Buchanans' *Osprey*, the Cataldis' *Carmelletta*, the McClouds' *Tartan Lady*, the Lorens' *Gladstone Belle*, Whip's *Sweet Heather*, and the Steeles' *Seeker*. All gone.

Far up from the jetties and sheds, the tea-tree path

thinned and, having passed through the banksias, opened into a broad expanse of sand. Here were the remains of the mangroves, where Rachel's mother and Miriam Burgess had seen . . . but what they had seen she would not think about or try to imagine, and far over, beyond this, was the lantana, where Rachel would not go.

Now, hesitating among the trees at the end of the path, she saw the motorbike on the other side of the clearing. Beside it was a small tent of blue plastic and, below the bank, the stranger she had seen in the town.

Good, she thought, and stepped back a little.

As she moved, quiet as she was, two white herons lifted from among the branches.

He looked up at once. "Hey," he said. "Is someone there?"

The birds circled, their wings spread wide, showing bright yellow beneath.

"Hey," he said again and pulled himself up to the level of the sand. "I know someone's there."

Cautiously she stepped out of the trees.

"I thought there was someone," he said, straightening up and brushing sand from his hands. "I saw those birds take off."

She kept still, saying nothing.

He stood at the edge of the bank, looking up. "They're big, aren't they?"

"They're herons," she said. "They nest there every year."

"Ah." He nodded.

He had changed out of his coat and jeans and wore a white T-shirt, the same as hers, and gray shorts. He was as tall as she was, his skin and hair dark, his body lithe and sinewy, which she liked.

He lifted his arm and wiped sweat from his forehead. "It's hot here. I think the bank cuts the breeze."

"The wind comes off the water," she said. "It should be cooler down there."

His face was lean, his bone structure prominent. "Sculpted," Sarah would have said.

He grinned a crooked grin. "You know a lot about this place," he said, walking toward her.

She stepped back. Tucked in the waistband of his shorts was the pick, glinting silver.

He saw the trouble. "Don't worry," he said, holding it out to her with the handle across his palm, like a peace offering. "It's a geologist's pick. I'm digging down there, at the face of the bank."

She looked straight into his face. She had grown up among men.

"This is a midden," he said. "This whole area." He spread his arms wide, and the new metal of the pick head glinted in the sun.

"What's a midden?"

"A midden? You're standing on one."

She looked down to her bare feet, then back at him as if he were mad. He could tell what she was thinking.

"A midden is a great pile of shells. Millions of them, packed down layer on layer, then covered in sand or whatever. Maybe dirt and grass. Here it's still mostly sand." He kicked the ground. He was not wearing shoes either. Over his feet and up to his ankles was a thick coating of black mud. He had been standing in the mud below the bank.

"Shells?" she said. "There aren't any decent shells around here. If you're looking for shells, you'd do better on the surf beach, over those sandhills." She pointed toward the sea. "But mostly they're no good. They get broken on the reefs, a long way out. The ones that are washed in are usually broken."

He shook his head and, putting down the pick, dropped to his knees. "No. I don't mean that sort of shell. Not really seashells." He dug in the sand with his fingers. "I mean these. Oyster shells, like these." He held out his hands. Scattered amongst the sand he had scooped up were pieces of bleached shell, old and brittle. "These are the kinds of shells you find in a midden. Oyster shells. They're all over the place here. Right where we are standing."

She realized immediately what he meant. He was still looking up at her, his hands extended, so she moved closer and knelt facing him. "I never take any notice of these. They're from the mangrove beds."

"Sure," he said, "but not recently. These could be thousands of years old."

He tipped some of the sand into her palm. "These are the leftovers from Aboriginal feasts, over who knows how many hundreds or thousand of years. That's what forms a midden. Lots of Aborigines at a clambake."

"A clambake?"

"That's what the Yanks would call it. Sounds better than an oyster party. But that's what it was."

"You're not American," she said, "are you?"

"Me? I'm not anything."

"Me either," she said. "Except an Australian. I was born here in New Canaan."

He sat down, his legs out in front, very near to brushing hers. "I'm Sam Shadows," he said, "and don't say anything about my name. It's mine and I'm stuck with it. I'm studying anthropology at the university. This digging is part of my fieldwork."

Rachel laughed. "There aren't too many fields around New Canaan."

"No," he said, "not like wheat fields. I mean outside work. Practical work. I had to do a survey of an archaeological site for an assignment. This place was mentioned in one of my reference books. It said that there was a major oyster midden here, but so far as I could tell, no one has ever studied it in any detail.

There was only that one mention of the midden site, then nothing else. That happens. Someone turns up a queer rock or bone when they're digging in their backyard, they do the right thing and send it in to a museum for identification, but it gets put to one side and forgotten for years. I guess that's what happened here. Someone came across this place once and made a note of it, but no one came back to follow up."

She could think of nothing to say. She dropped her eyes from his and realized what had been happening; that they were sitting there, facing each other on the sand, out in the open.

"I think I had better be going," she said, getting up.

He drew his legs in and stood too, reaching for the pick as he did so. "Do you live near here?" he said.

She nodded, turning to go. She didn't especially want to answer questions, but he went on.

"Are you a student, or do you work?"

"I work," she said.

He was not satisfied. "Where? In the city?"

"I help my father with his catch. He's a fisherman down here." She was walking backward as she spoke and was certain that his face changed. He would hardly be impressed, looking as good as he did and being a university student.

Then he said, "What about your name?"

When she told him, still walking backward, he said, "Well, Rachel, for a local you're in an awful hurry. I could show you what I'm doing if you like."

She needed to get away. "I can't stay," she said and was instantly sorry. No girl in a magazine behaved like this.

She was almost into the cover of the trees.

He called out, "I'll be here tomorrow. And probably every weekend for the next two months." He was shouting by this time.

Once among the trees, she turned to look back. She was certain that he could not see her. He was standing as she had left him, the pick still glinting in his hand.

III

On the following Wednesday, the girls turned sixteen. Rachel's father gave her a gold chain and heart-shaped locket which had belonged to her mother. The locket was hinged to open and might hold a lock of hair or a photograph. At the time it was empty, but she was happy that he had remembered. With her mother gone, she had been certain that the day would be forgotten.

This happened to Sarah. First thing that morning she went to the jetty, upended a crate, and started the sort. She worked quickly.

"My brother reckons that I look like a whale in these," she said pointing to the navy bib-and-brace overalls she had taken to wearing. "I said that was a compliment."

Rachel was not fooled. She waited for the silence that she knew would come—that came every morning—and said, "Did they forget?"

Sarah nodded. "And you?"

With her little finger Rachel hooked the chain from beneath her shirt. The locket flashed in the sun.

"It would be hard for me to forget," she said. "But you will have to wait. I didn't want to give you anything down here. Come over after four."

"I will," Sarah said.

When the boats had gone out, they sat together on Rachel's back verandah and waited for the night wind.

"Anything?" Rachel asked.

Sarah shook her head. "They never said a word. I thought that one of them might have left something for me to find. You know, a sort of surprise. Joseph likes that sort of joke. But I've been all over the house, cleaning up bits and pieces, and there's nothing."

"From me," Rachel said, and took an envelope from the back pocket of her jeans. "See?" She pulled her chair closer. "It's a voucher for a book club. I filled in your name and address. And there's the money order for the subscription. I did it through the store and pre-paid for three months. I'll pay the rest as they come. It's all done for you. All you have to do is check off the books that you want and post it."

Sarah looked up, smiling. "This is terrific, thanks. But what about this money? It's got here that this costs fifteen dollars a month."

"I can use some from the housekeeping. They're hardcover books, so it's good value. There's an introductory gift too. Read out what it says on the back."

"It says: 'This book club is designed to suit all reading interests, from eight to eighty, from fact to fantasy.' And then there's a list of authors and titles to pick from. I wouldn't need to pick. I would read whatever they sent. Thanks, Rachel."

She dug into the bib pocket of her overalls and held out her hand. "Here's something for you."

Rachel looked in disbelief. In Sarah's palm lay a roll of money, a gray rubber band wound around it. She could see a twenty and beneath that a ten, at least one.

"I can't take that," she said. "When they find out at home, they'll kill you." She put her hands behind her back.

Sarah laughed. "You think I pinched it, do you? You think I took it out of Dad's tobacco tin? Or Joseph's drinking money? Well, I didn't. You don't think I'd give you something I stole, do you?"

Ignoring the hand extended to her, Rachel got up and turned to the screens.

"Nothing would surprise me anymore," she said, pressing her fingers against the rough mesh. "But there must be fifty dollars there at least."

"Actually there's one hundred and seventy-six."

"What? A hundred and seventy-six dollars? Where could you get that?"

"In our house . . ."

"Then it's your father's and your brother's. It's from the catch. It's depot money. It isn't mine."

Sarah sighed. She stuffed the notes in her bib pocket and pulled herself up to stand behind Rachel. "Did I hear 'Thanks for the money, Sarah. Thanks for my birthday present'? No, I didn't. What do you take me for? An idiot? Have I ever stolen a thing in my life? Have I?"

Rachel said nothing.

" 'No'? Do I hear 'No'? If you can't answer, you can look at me."

She took Rachel's elbow, turning her around. "Now, listen. I found the money. And I can tell you how if you give me five minutes. Since it's my birthday . . ."

"Our birthday."

"OK. Our birthday. Are we all right now? Are we all over our little fit of temper?"

Rachel nodded.

"Good. Then, listen. My mother is still not speaking, not to Dad or Joseph or me. She hasn't even cleaned the church or done the Father's place. I try to make contact. I pretend nothing is wrong. I talk about anything. And I read to her every night. That's what they do in hospitals if someone is in a coma. They say that something goes in. Something registers in the subconscious. So the other night I got her Bible like I do and I read that piece out of the book of Ezekiel where the prophet sees the valley full of dry bones and the bones come together and rise up . . ."

"You read to your mother about the valley of dry bones?"

"You remember the part?"

"I remember the Father telling it . . ."

"Then, shush. Just listen. You know how it says that one day these bones rise up and come back together to form bodies with flesh and blood and how they will all live again in the Kingdom of God? I read that part, then I stopped and put the Bible down. I usually do that. I read some, then try to talk to her. I said to her straight out that she might as well be one of the skeletons in that pile of bones for all the good that she was doing sitting around day after day. I said it was no good and I wanted to know when it would be over. How long did she need before she was going to forget whatever it was she was thinking about and become a real living person again? I told her that all the sitting and all the moping in the world wouldn't bring back your mum, if that was what it was all about. I said that I meant nothing to her. That I'm . . ."

Rachel cut her off. She turned from where she had been staring out. "Don't say that," she said. "It's rubbish and you know it. Besides, you make it sound like it's your fault that she's gone the way she has. It's not. It's got nothing to do with you. Something has happened in her head that we don't know about. Something queer . . ."

She changed her tone and, dropping her voice, pressed her palms against the screens. "But I don't see what any of this has to do with that money."

"You promised that you'd listen. So be quiet and listen. Don't comment. I said those things because maybe if I was different she would pull out of it. Maybe . . ."

"Different? How different?"

"I wanted her to be proud of me. I wanted her to look at me and listen to me. Like she did with your mother. As if I was her friend. Not a child. Not a little girl. I said that to her. I said all the things that I just said to you. Next thing, I see her move her hand—she hasn't moved when I'm reading or talking, not once—and she wiped her face. Her cheek. She's crying. See? I said, 'Mum, Mum,' and I got down on the floor next to her and grabbed hold of her hand. I said, 'Mum. I'm right here next to you.' Then she put her hand on top of my head and patted my hair, and she said as plain as you like, 'Get out. Go. There's danger here. Take the money in the pantry. At the back.' That's all she said; then next thing, she got up and went into the house. Into her bedroom."

Rachel looked at her, waiting.

"It's true. Every word of it. She talked—that's the first time since your mother died. 'Get out. Go. There's danger here,' she said, as if she knew something. And her eyes were wide as wide, exactly like she was seeing something—not me, not in my face—but behind me, something in the bush, way over, toward the core. I didn't do anything. Just sat there. When I heard her bedroom door shut, I did what she said. I went into the pantry, to the back, and started looking. I didn't even know what I was looking for. Not really. And anyway, I've been doing the cooking for so long that if anybody knew what was in the pantry, it was me. The canisters and tins—all that stuff—I dug around and looked behind things, but there was nothing, and I started losing my temper and crying. I thought that she might have been getting back at me for something, or teaching me a lesson, but I couldn't work out why. Anyway, I took everything out of the pantry and put it on the kitchen floor, but there was nothing. So I left the whole mess and went to bed. Then about three the next morning, I woke up and I just knew. All that was left in that pantry were the shelves, and Mum had put layer after layer of newspapers on them. That's all she ever used the paper for. Lining the pantry shelves. I went straight in, but there was nothing beneath the paper, but in it, between the layers. That's where the money was. Buried between these layers of newspaper. So it is mine, because she told me to have it. And if it's mine, then I can give it to you. See? It's a long story but . . ."

"But what are we supposed to do? Take the money and leave? I don't get what you're saying. We can't just leave. I couldn't do that."

"Mum said, 'Get out.' That's what she said. She didn't say it horribly. Not at all. She said it like a last wish, if that makes sense. Like I would be better off gone. She hasn't said anything else since. Not a word. So I want you to keep the money. I don't mean that we go right away. Nothing like that. I can't leave her, that's for sure. I could leave the others. They would drink themselves to death and not even miss me. But not her. All I want is to know that it's there, safe somewhere, if we need it. If we have to get out. So take it. It's our birthday present. Even if one of us could go. See? If there was a chance for one to get out. Like you. I would be all right. I would be all right here with my books. OK? Rachel . . ."

Rachel had a finger to her lips. She stood staring into the twilight yard.

"What?" Sarah whispered. "What?"

Then the Angel appeared at the foot of the stairs.

"I came to say happy birthday," he said. "The Father told me. But I waited a while when I seen you were busy talking."

"And I seen you standing waiting. And I seen you

listening too," Rachel said, mimicking him.

With a sign for Sarah to follow, she went into the darkened house.

IV

The next Saturday, as soon as she had finished sorting, Rachel said, "Sarah, you go on. I'm not going back to the house yet. The herons are nesting in the banksias. I'm going down for a look."

She took the tea-tree path, and at the edge of the clearing she looked across, and there was the bike and the blue tent. But there was no movement, except for the occasional flutter from the herons in the trees behind, and all about hung the silence of the lagoon.

She didn't doubt that the boy was there— somewhere—and walked straight to his camp to see. Outside the tent, at her feet, a neat pile of driftwood was stacked by the ashes of an earlier fire, and there was a bright new billycan for making tea, a jerrycan of water, a couple of tins of baked beans, an enamel plate, an enamel cup, a spoon and can opener, the pick she had seen the week before, a shovel, a trowel, a paintbrush and, neatly arranged in a black leather case which she stooped to pick up and unzipped carefully, silver instruments, the same as those the dentist used when he came from the city in his mobile clinic.

With a fingertip she tested the sharpness of their hooks and barbs; she thought of her mother, of the puncture of the skin that had taken her forever. The case bothered her. She closed it and knelt to replace it, but as she did, she noticed that the flap of the tent was open and looked in.

Inside was bare except for an unrolled sleeping bag, and immediately she felt the closeness of the plastic and the heat of the trapped air against her face. There was a hazy light too, like the heat haze that shimmered above the sand at midday, but not the same, because this light was a queer underwater blue that she had seen before, although where, exactly, she could not think.

It was so unbearably hot that she had begun to back out—she was on her hands and knees—when she heard someone laughing and turned to see Sam behind her, looking down. She felt like a fool, but he quite naturally put out his hand to help her up.

"Sorry I wasn't here," he said. "I was up at that headland and I looked down and saw you come out of the trees. I came back as fast as I could."

She got up, brushing the sand off her jeans and, pushing the locket inside her shirt, tried her best to cover her embarrassment.

"I was looking in your tent. I thought . . ." She could not finish. What she had been doing was obvious.

"It's OK," he said. "I was wondering if you would

come back. I looked out for you last Sunday too. It sure is lonely here, especially after dark. Last Saturday night was an awful long night."

She nodded toward a kerosene lamp hooked over the tent pole. "You've got a light. Did you use that?"

"Not yet. I only camped here that one night. Last Saturday. While there was still some daylight, I made my dinner." He nudged a can of beans with his foot. "Then just at dark I went for a walk through the sandhills and out along the surf beach. I thought I would come back and read for a while in the tent, but I ended up making a fire and sitting near that. This place was giving me the willies."

She nodded, not knowing what else to do.

"But tonight will be different," he was saying. "Tonight I'll probably use the lamp. I should have turned up enough info to start making notes. I want to do some drawings too. Some sketches . . ."

He knelt beside the opening to the tent and, slipping his hand through, lifted out a folder.

"I kept this under the sleeping bag, where that instrument case should have been put. You probably didn't notice this one though."

She felt her face burn; he must have seen everything.

"I keep my notes in this," he said. "I get them down rough, then put them in order later. And then I do the sketches."

He held out the open folder to show her what he

had done—lines and figures and symbols that meant nothing to her. She understood little of what he was talking about either, though she guessed this was something to do with his work on the midden. She pointed to a row of drawings, each roughly oval in shape.

"Are they oyster shells?"

He laughed, but it was not a laugh intended to ridicule.

"Great. At least someone can recognize what they are. I was thinking they looked like little turds . . ."

He stopped, realizing what he had said, and turned toward the bank of the lagoon.

"Sorry," he said without looking at her. "I didn't mean to say that. I could show you what the sketches are. What I'm doing, I mean, if you would come down here."

And still without turning he walked toward the bank.

She followed him, saying nothing. At the edge he turned as if to help her down, but she jumped, and still at the top, he shrugged, then copied her.

The bank was quite high here, a little over their heads.

"This is where I've been working," he said, pointing to the top.

She could see grass roots exposed and some that were black and thick, spreading from the scrub farther back. "The bank has been formed by the tide cutting into the sand. It must have been the high winter tides, because there's not enough water about now to cut out the sand like this."

"But you've dug some of that," she said. "It's not just the tide."

He nodded and reached up, scooping out loose sand with his fingers.

"I've dug a lot of this out. You see, I worked this piece, one yard wide, from top to bottom. A strip. From the ground level with the grass, down to the waterline . . . and the mud."

She looked down and laughed. Their feet were settling in the ooze.

"Anyway. That's what I'm doing, and you can see the layers of shells. Look. A layer of shell, a layer of sand, a layer of shell, another one of sand . . . and that's how it goes, down the strip. It's like a cake—the layers in a slice of cake."

She understood what he meant straight off, but he seemed determined to go on.

"These are stratified layers; they might be anywhere from three inches to three yards deep—that just depends how big the Aborigines' feast was, or where they got into the habit of chucking their empty shells, or even whether it was a good year for oysters or not. But here." He pointed again, "This stuff is charcoal. See? It runs right along the bank. There must have been a big fire here once. A bush fire that went right over the top.

"You can't burn shell," she said. "A fire couldn't have burned right over the top if it was shell."

He walked a little along the bank, found a thick root, and hauled himself up. When he reached down for her hand, she accepted, and he lifted her and walked with her to the tent.

"No, you can't burn shell," he said. "Except under terrific heat, like they do to make lime. But over the years those shell heaps would have been covered in sand, blown there by the wind or dumped there by the tide, and then ground covers would grow, grasses and vines, and after that the bush. Like that tea-tree patch where you come from. Maybe the midden goes all the way up under there too. Even under that thick stuff over there."

He pointed to the lantana.

"I don't feel like getting caught in that, but that's what I have to find out. Where this midden begins and ends. The extent of it."

"Your drawings and notes," she said, "is that what they're all about?"

They were at the tent, and he sat on the sand, opening the folder and holding it out to her.

"Sit down. I'll show you. These lines I've drawn here are the layers of shells I've counted in that strip of bank. Six layers in all, from the present surface, the one you walk on, the tea-tree level, you could call it, down to the bottom, or mud level, the black-feet level. The shells could go deeper. I would have to sink a trench to find out. That's all part of my assignment. To find the full extent of the midden—its depth and area. But also"—and he turned his pages—"I want to find out the content of the deposits, what's buried in each layer, to find out what the Aborigines ate. The types of shellfish. That's why I did those oyster shell drawings. For identification. But sometimes in the shell you can turn up other things, mixed in. Things the people lost or threw away, like tools for opening the shells, or the tips of fishing spears, or even bones . . ."

He reached back inside the tent and produced a clear plastic bag. "Like this . . ." And he tipped the bag so that a fragile, white splinter of bone dropped into his palm.

"This is a queer one. Not like a shell or fish bone."

"It's a bone from the tail of a stingray," she said. "The lagoon's full of stingrays. They lie flat on the bottom, in the shallowest parts, so they can get the sun. That's a stingray bone."

He looked at her in admiration. "What are these, then?" he said, undoing the button-down flap of his shirt pocket and holding out a pile of shells and other bits and pieces. "Can you tell what these are?"

"That's part of the skull of a flathead, and that's just the lower half of a spanner crab's nipper, that's a shark's tooth—a big shark too—and look . . ." She picked at the tooth with her fingernail until a little piece of hardened sand fell away. "There's a hole been put through it."

She held it up for him to see, and he took it from her, amazed.

"It is a hole. It's been drilled, like part of a necklace or even a charm for around the neck."

He looked at her again. "The piece I thought was important is worth nothing, but this thing I stuck in my pocket is . . . You're great. You should be doing this course, not me. You know that?"

She was embarrassed. She said, "You're laughing at me, aren't you? I know all that because I see those things up there on the jetty every day of my life. Anyone in New Canaan could recognize a shark's tooth. That's not so hard. Besides, there are plenty of people who have been closer to the real thing than me."

"Caught one, you mean?"

"And been taken. Like Thomas Whip, who owned the *Sweet Heather*. His shed is still up there, past those mangroves. He was bringing in his nets one night, using the winch, when there was a snare, and the winch fouled and stopped. He thought he had fouled the screw—that the net was caught in the boat's propeller—and he was leaning over the stern to see, when up came a white pointer. A shark. It must have lifted clear of the surface—Tom would have pulled back, of course—but too late, because the thing clamped its jaws on his arm just above the elbow. He screamed out, and his helper came and grabbed him around the middle and pulled him back so they fell onto the deck. But Tom's arm was gone. Well, not altogether. The bite had stripped all the flesh, right back to the bone, and the hand was gone. They say that it happened so fast Tom never even realized. Anyway, he died right there on the deck, but when they brought him up to our house so that my mother and her friend Mrs. Burgess could lay him out, they found there were still shark teeth embedded in his arm, or what was left of it, the flesh above the elbow. My mother said that the Father took the teeth, but I have never seen them myself."

"Your father took the teeth?"

"No. The Father. The priest here."

"You call him the Father?"

"Or Gray Eye."

"Gray Eye?"

"Sometimes we call him that. Because of the kids' rhyme, you know:

> "Black-eyed beauty
> Do your father's duty,
> Gray-eye greedy gut
> Eat all the . . ."

She stopped, afraid that she was making a fool of herself.

"Finish it," he said. "I never heard of it. Go on."

"*Eat all the world up.* That's the last line. *Gray-eye greedy gut, eat all the world up.*"

For a moment he said nothing. Then, "This father, is he old? Has he been here for years?"

"Since the beginning," she said, getting to her feet. "Why?"

He stood also but did not answer. When they were face to face, he said, "Will you help me here? You know about this area. Could you come down and help me?"

She was uncomfortable. She put her hand to her throat and felt the locket there.

"Maybe," she said, "but I have to go now. My dad will be awake, and I'll have to do his lunch."

She began walking across the clearing, and as he had the week before, he called after her.

"I'll be here tomorrow. I have to leave about one. Could you come back before then?"

She was already thinking, *Sarah, Sarah, what have I started?* and wondering if she could ever tell.

In the center of the clearing, she stopped and turned.

"I go to church on Sundays," she said. "In the morning . . ." And then came a voice that she could not believe was her own: "I might see you after that."

She heard him call, "Good-bye, Rachel."

But she did not turn again or answer.

V

In the morning Rachel arrived at Sarah's place as usual and waited for her by the screen door at the back. When Sarah made her appearance, grimacing and hitching and tugging at the pink gingham dress that her mother had made especially for Sundays —Pollyanna's Revenge, Rachel called it—the girls walked together to the church.

Once, when things were different, their mothers had walked with them. But never their fathers, sleeping off the night before; they had their own service. Every Sunday, as darkness fell, the Father would take the path to the depot jetty, and there, framed against the great nets strung tremulous in the first whispers of night wind, he would meet with the men alone.

"It must be the Blessing of the Fleet," Sarah would say. "What else could it be?"

Rachel could not imagine. Nor could she understand the purpose of the service of women, held at the church each Sunday. But she went. She knew the consequences for those who did not.

Now the girls turned out from among the houses— Rachel smart in white and Sarah protesting in pink —and before them, across the track, the Father's garden and the church rose up from the drab scattering of sand and scrub like a view selected for a postcard. Since the scrub and swamp surrounding New Canaan yielded very little timber suited to building and the only stone was basalt, gray and unsightly, the walls of the church were constructed entirely of pine packing cases which had once contained, among other cargo, blocks and tackle and bilge pumps and ship's engines and all that was required to harvest the sea, and drills and cutting blades and winches and derricks to extract the stone from the core. And since these cases were short in supply and high in demand, the church boasted a single skin only, being entirely unlined. To protect it from the elements—not only rain and wind, but sea salt also, driven up by the wind—the pine had been coated with layer upon layer of marine varnish, so that the walls of the church seemed golden. And as the shingles of the roof were of basalt, cut thin as slate, they served as hosts to the encrusting salt, which sparkled like crystal by day, and by moonlight was lustrous silver.

But as the Father had insisted that there be a spire, with the weight of the shingles, the pressure on the wall bearers was so great that buttresses were needed. Rough blocks of basalt were mortared upward, one on top of the other, almost to the eaves, to contain the bulging. The lime for this mortar had come from oyster shells, burned at great heat.

The Father's church was a marvelous place. So too was his garden.

From a single gateway in its pumice wall a path of crushed shells led directly to the church door. Either side of this, and stretching to the very limits of the enclosure, the Father's garden was dense with blooms. Low down, in beds edged in lumps of pumice daubed white, thrived iris in both blue and purple, and there was the yellow of calla lilies with their lush leaves, and higher the fragile pink of hollyhocks, staked tall to resist even a suggestion of the sea, but above these, or bursting from among them, were red and white roses and citrus of all kinds, pruned severely into spheres, yet thick with flowers or heavy with fruit.

Once, when the girls were much younger and waiting for their mothers to finish cleaning, Sarah had said to Rachel, "You could find a unicorn in this garden. Or a little dragon with a blue dorsal fin raised like a sail."

Rachel laughed. "Fish have dorsal fins," she said, "and I can't see any fish walking about here."

Now as the girls entered the gate and their Sunday shoes crunched the shells beneath them, it was no walking fish or dorsaled dragon that stepped out of the garden to block their way, but the Angel in his borrowed suit.

"Good morning, Rachel," he said, standing steady, his hands in his pockets, his feet placed wide. "How does it feel to be sixteen?"

Rachel was not ready for him. She had seen him here before, working in the garden, but not on a Sunday, never at this time. And all morning she had been congratulating herself on the night before. How painlessly, how smartly she had got rid of him.

She looked at him, lost for words.

"Angel," Sarah said, putting herself forward, "you know you could have asked me the same question."

He ignored her, looking over her head at Rachel. "Well," he said, "can I have an answer?"

"It feels much the same as being fifteen," she said. "And that was all right."

"Yes," he said. "Fifteen was all right."

Then, as if he could contain it no longer, he blurted, "The Father said I could come. I'm going to sit with you."

But she was too fast for him. Grabbing at some protruding piece of Sarah's gingham, she pushed him aside and walked directly down the path and through the door into the church.

Instead of taking their usual pew at the back against the wall, she dragged Sarah toward the altar and shoved her into a pew before it.

"Spread your dress out," she whispered, her breath hot on Sarah's ear. "Take up all the seat."

Hardly had she spoken than the figure of the Father appeared.

There was no organ in the church at New Canaan, and no choir or pulpit either, nothing but a stark slab of basalt which served as an altar, positioned squarely at the end of the aisle. On the floor before this the Father stood to deliver his sermon, which he now began without further ceremony.

Sarah was in a state of confusion. She was pushed into an unfamiliar pew, her cheeks still burning from the humiliation of being dragged the entire length of the aisle. Twisting around and peering between the stony-faced women who sat staring back at her, she checked on the whereabouts of the Angel, and satisfied that he had not entered the church, she ignored the Father and quite deliberately turned to examine the pale wood of the packing-case wall. Here was some recompense—a new pew brought different cargo—and she was soon thoroughly engrossed in deciphering the cryptic remains of the directions and labels and trademarks punched or stamped or burned on the timber beside her.

Nor was Rachel listening to the service. She guessed that somewhere behind her the Angel was waiting—although, unlike Sarah, she would not turn to make sure—and she sat rigid, staring at her hands clenched in her lap, contemplating how best to make her exit, or escape, once the Father had finished.

Then, vaguely at first, she grew aware of the color of her hands. They were blue. She flattened her fingers and smoothed her skirt. She looked again. Her skirt was dappled blue. She turned her palms up. She saw her forearms, her knees, her legs.

I am blue all over, she thought, *the same as in that tent,* and she looked up, fascinated.

She saw the answer at once. She had not sat in this

pew before, never this close to the front, and spilling down upon her—and Sarah too, with her lolly-pink gingham turned to purple—was the blue light from the fisherman's window, set high above the altar.

The window was a circle of colored glass, not one piece, but hundreds, each irregular in shape and crudely set in lead. No professional artisan had made this. The people of New Canaan had worked at it themselves, gathering broken jars and bottles or, where they could find nothing better, lumps of china. But the predominant glass was blue, mostly from medicine bottles, and against this background, which could have been sea or sky, there stood a man in robes of white.

This was the fisherman. His arms were opened wide and appeared at first to welcome or to offer a gesture of embrace. But this was an illusion. From his fingers hung a net of lead, and caught in it were tiny creatures, men and women and children, some of china, black against the light. Two women knelt at his feet, and across the drapery over their knees was a great book. One held a feather and the other a jar, suggesting that these women were scribes, recording the names of the captives in the net.

Now Rachel looked closely at the two women and saw, or thought she saw, another face between theirs.

She leaned forward.

"What?" Sarah whispered. "What?"

"Nothing," Rachel breathed, staring.

Then she was sure. What she had always taken for folds and tucks in the fisherman's robe was a face.

Sarah saw her sit back suddenly.

"What?" she said again.

At that moment there was movement and the women dropped to their knees.

The murmured liturgy began:

> "Father, guide us,
> Guide us in the paths;
> Father, guide us,
> Guide us all our lives."

On the "Amen," the service was over, and as the Father moved up the aisle to take his place at the entrance, Sarah said, "What is going on? Are you sick? Tell me!"

Without a word Rachel stood and headed for the door. She made it past the Father, with the briefest of nods, and onto the path, but she could go no farther. The Angel was waiting at the gate.

"Get out of my way," she said, attempting to push by, but he would not have it and caught her about the waist, spinning her around to face him.

"Who do you think you are?" he said. "I came to see you last night and you laughed at me. I came here for you today, the only man here, and you walk past me like I'm bloody nothing. So are you too good for me? Hey?"

She shook herself free, but he came after her and caught her again, this time by the arm. Without hesitation she spun around, hitting him across the face with her open palm, so that he staggered back.

"Get!" she said. "Once and for all. Get!"

Then she ran.

From behind, among the women, Sarah saw everything.

And from the shadow of the porch, the Father had seen too.

VI

Sarah walked home alone, her thoughts only of Rachel and the trouble with the Angel. In one way or another the "I'm going to make you mine" thing had been going on for years. It was time Rachel belted him one. And it was time that the Father saw exactly how she felt. For sure he was the one who was behind it all, encouraging the Angel and setting them up. Or setting Rachel up. As if the Angel was a stud bull or a breeding stallion. And what did that make Rachel? She thought about this, sometimes talking to herself aloud, sometimes stopping dead in the middle of the path, but all the while undoing bows and tugging at ribbons so that by the time she reached her own screen door, she had all but stepped out of her Sunday dress.

She checked on her mother, sitting staring in her cane chair, changed into overalls, and got on with making the lunch. The men would be stirring soon.

In the afternoon she sat by her mother and read, sometimes to her, sometimes not.

Later she made up the dinners for the night. When the men had gone, she did the dishes, showered, made sure her mother had a bath, made sure her mother ate something, ate something herself, then sat on the verandah and listened to the radio, waiting for Rachel.

But Rachel did not come.

In the morning, when Sarah said, "Well, where were you last night?" Rachel would not answer, at least not to Sarah's satisfaction.

"Leave me alone" was all she could say.

Sarah did, finishing the sort in silence.

The same silence came down the next day and the next, and on Saturday morning Sarah left the jetty in tears and walked the path to her house alone. Worse, when she came to open the screen door, there on the top step was a parcel—Slattery from the store delivered the mail anytime and anywhere that he liked—and she guessed that it contained the first title from the book club that Rachel had subscribed to for her birthday only the week before.

Her mother was on the verandah, sitting the

way she did, and Sarah took the parcel into her bedroom.

This was a special place, the center of Sarah's world. The story went that it was the captain's cabin from a wool clipper, the *Liberty*, that had run aground to the north of the lagoon; that the Old Man—her great-grandfather—had ripped it out complete before the surf beat the vessel to splinters. Her father said that the entire house had been built around this cabin and that the Old Man had intended to use it as his private retreat, but when the house was finished, he would not enter it, maintaining that he had heard the panels groan, had seen them bow and shudder, and though the timbers of the *Liberty* lay bleached and worm-riddled upon the beaches of the earth, the cabin alone remained, "her heart," he said, beating yet on dark and unseen waters.

Sarah's father believed this, and so did her brother, but from childhood she had not, gladly taking the cabin as her room and delighting in the privacy that its mystery assured.

The walls were paneled in cedar, glowing in the richest, deepest red. At the release of two brass clamps, a panel could be lowered, and there was the bed, fitted with a valance of calico, and a net, draped like a sail, which could be dropped or drawn depending on the sleeper's mood. There were also cabinets of cedar, tall and glass fronted, which once housed the *Liberty*'s library—"wonderful books," the Old Man said, "bound in leather and trimmed in gold: books of the sea, of Antipodean lands, of the stars and planets and the firmament beyond: books of poetry and people"—but every volume had been lost, so the story went, washed from the deck during salvage, and now the shelves were empty, except for the few books that Sarah owned, well thumbed and tatty.

The external wall of the cabin was a great bay window which provided an uninterrupted view of the ocean, and in this enclosure of glass, on a circular rug of bright, woven rag, there squatted a leather chair—the captain's chair—its winged back and scrolled arms offering a permanent invitation to curl up and dream.

Into this sanctuary Sarah flopped, and with one quick glance through the window—as if to make sure that the sea was still there—she opened the parcel. Inside was an envelope and a letter welcoming her to the club. It said that her first book would arrive shortly; it was hoped that she could make good use of her introductory gift, included at no extra charge. Sarah opened the envelope. There was a book, but not exactly the type she had supposed. This had no dust jacket, no title or author, just a plain black cardboard cover. There was no print. Not a word. Inside was blank paper. She turned to the front, then the back. The endpapers were marbled in green and gold. It was a notebook. She opened it at the center, lifted it to smell, then rested it on her knees and spread her palms flat over it, rubbing, to feel the new paper.

She was satisfied. She would use it—for sure—but how she did not know. Lifting it against her chest, she slipped down dreaming into the depths of the chair.

VII

Am I mad? Rachel asked herself as she watched Sarah leave the jetty that morning. *Have I gone stupid? Have I gone stupid like her mother, not talking to anybody?*

For a week she had sat there, working in silence, saying nothing except what was necessary to complete the sort. It was impossible for her to talk. How could she? How could she tell Sarah about Sam; the way he made her feel? How could she make sense of what she had seen in the church—the face in the folds of the fisherman's dress, or gown, or whatever it was—and the sea-blue light falling on her, changing the color of her skin? These things didn't happen to her. They might happen to Sarah, or Sarah might imagine them happening, and spin them into stories that made her laugh and say, "No more!"

But what had happened with Sam was real. He had walked his bike into that town as calm as you like.

One look at him and she knew that he was smart, not like a local. Not at all like the Angel. And she had gone down and talked to him as easy as pie. Then there was the way he talked to her and how he stood or sat next to her or touched her with or without meaning to. All this made her think. It was the reason she had seen his face in the church. Or thought that she had seen it. Hidden in the folds of the fisherman's . . . *I must be off my head*, she thought. *A boy talks to me like I'm a human being and I start to see things.*

But she had every intention of seeing him again. She went directly to her house, showered, brushed her hair, slipped into a fresh shirt and jeans, then headed down the tea-tree path.

As soon as she saw his bike, she called out, and he scrambled over the bank.

"Well," he said, with his crooked grin, "the incredible vanishing woman. Where did you get to last Sunday?"

"Something happened," she said, remembering with a twinge of guilt that Sarah had asked the same question and had still not been given an answer. "I was going to come back."

"I waited. I didn't leave here until three, and all because of you I got home after dinner."

As he spoke, he wagged an accusing finger at her, but she could see that he was not serious.

"Serves you right for relying on people you don't

know," she said. "Were you in trouble from your parents?"

"From my parents?" He laughed and walked back toward the bank. "I live on campus at the university. I'm not likely to get into trouble. I missed my dinner at the dining room, that's all."

"So where are your parents?" she said, walking after him.

"Dead, I think."

"I'm sorry," she said, then added, as if to compensate: "I've only got a dad myself. I have to do the house for him and be there when he wants. I can't . . ." She was going to say "get away," but thought better of it and changed her tone. "Anyway, have you done any digging?"

"Sure," he said. "A fair bit. If I go on at this rate, I'll be finished in a couple more weeks." They were at the edge of the bank. He jumped down and turned with his hand out, ready to help her do the same. She stepped back.

"I can get down OK," she said, and jumped.

Later, when he had shown her more of his dig at the bank, he spread a plastic sheet outside his tent, and on that he opened the folder of notes she had seen the week before. He flicked over pages of measurements and sketches, explaining as he turned, but he need not have—this time she could recognize at once what he had done. Before her were drawings of the midden strata, a different shading for each layer he had identified.

"These are the field drawings that I said I had to do. They're still only rough, but you can make out what I mean. I scribble down the measurements as I go along, then I do them properly, to scale, back at the university. You can see here where I found something—like a different shell—in amongst the oysters or the ash."

He pointed to a legend, the same as on a map, but here each letter identified an object and where it was found in the bank.

"I can tell the easy shells," he said, "like the cowries, but most others I can't, and I need to because they have to be drawn and identified. Anything unusual in the midden has to be properly recorded."

He flipped over the pages and removed a few sheets of graph paper, each showing an item drawn from different views. "I did those shells pretty roughly, but these are the things that matter most, the good stuff I didn't think I would be lucky enough to find."

He showed her drawings of rocks. "These are actual Aboriginal artifacts; the genuine article. Fantastic."

"They look like bits of rock," she said.

He reached into the tent and produced a bag of specimens, rocks again, the same as in the drawings. "No, they're more than rocks. An artifact is any . . ."

"I know what an artifact is," she said. "I did history."

"Ooops, sorry." He started putting the rocks back in the bag. "They reckon that once I get going, there's no shutting me up. You caught me just in time."

She said, "No. I didn't mean it that way," and put her hand out to stop him. "I meant that I know. I'm interested, not bored. If I was bored, I wouldn't be down here again."

Then she realized that she was touching him and how close he was. She pulled away and sat back.

He cleared his throat. "This is the sort of stuff that I've been studying at the university. And now I've found it down here. I'll show you."

He dug about in the bag and held out a piece of smooth red stone, chipped around the edges. "This is hand chipped," he said, "not natural. You can see that because the chips taken out are so even. And also, there are no stones like this about. It's not a local stone, it's been brought here. 'Introduced,' my lecturers would say, to be scientific. Maybe it was used to open shells or crack crabs' claws. See. I've drawn this one already. Always three views—a plan and two elevations. This one is small enough to draw full size. If it's too big for the page, then I scale it down."

He tipped it into Rachel's hand.

"You could photograph it," she said. "Why don't you do that? Take its photo against a sheet of white paper and save all the time?"

"You could. Some people do that. Proper arch-
aeologists. They photograph a big find, like a whole
skeleton, or say a big formation, like the foundation
of a building. They call that in situ photography,
but this stuff is only small. And besides, even if I
had that sort of gear, I couldn't bring it down here
and leave it around. It's too valuable. Security. You
need a buddy for that, someone always about your
camp. I just use the graph paper. It's economical, and
easy to cart around too. I trace around the thing,
like this."

He placed one of the chipped rocks on the page
over the drawing he had already made of it. "See. Or
if I have to, I can take measurements with callipers.
Have you seen callipers?"

She shook her head, and he reached for the instrument case she had unzipped the week before.

"These are callipers." Between his fingers he held a
pair of dividers, their chromed arms belled outward
from a central pin and coming together in two vicious
points.

"Don't jab yourself," he said. "They're sharp. I take
the measurements with them, then draw up whatever
it is, using the graph squares for proportion."

"It's detailed," she said. "Exact."

"That's the pencil. People usually draw with a soft
lead, but for this sort of thing you need something
that will stay very sharp. Hard graphite. You have to
be precise."

He was looking down at the paper. She had been listening but watching his face as he spoke. He sensed this and glanced up, catching her eye.

"You think I'm a big poser, don't you? Showing you all this stuff."

She shook her head. "No. I envy you. What you can do. The drawings. All you know."

He started packing things away, but he was smiling. "It's funny; you're the only person I've talked to since I first came here. And that's three weekends now. You're the only one."

"They mightn't be talking to you, but the locals would know you're here, don't worry. Some might know that I am too. It's that sort of town. You know. People snoop."

"And what about that Father? Does he snoop too?" He said this casually, without looking up.

"I guess. He always knows everything. I never thought . . . How come you ask that?"

"I wondered about him, that's all. If he ever mentions the Aborigines."

"Aborigines?" she said. "What Aborigines? There aren't any . . ."

He held his hand up, saying, "No. No. It's just that last time you called him Gray Eye. It sounded like an old busybody's name, that's all. I thought he might know something. A bit of local history, about what became of the people here. The midden people. Forget it. Listen, would you come and help at the dig?"

He turned as he spoke, lifting the tent flap to replace his folder, and as he bent low, the light from inside fell on his hair.

"Sam," she said, and when he turned to look back, his face lit from behind against that blue, there could be no doubt. This *was* the face in the window.

"What?" he said.

She stood up, brushing the sand from her knees. "I have to go," she said, not daring to look at him. "It's Saturday. I have to do Dad's lunch."

"Are you coming back this time?" As he spoke, he reached out and took her hand. Immediately she steadied herself, thinking, *This is it.*

She said, "If I do, can I bring a friend?"

She saw his face change. Her hand was released. "Your boyfriend?"

She laughed. "No. Don't be stupid. Only Sarah. My best friend all my life."

"Sure," he said, brightening. "Sure, she can come. If you tell me when, I'll even make a fire and boil the billycan."

"My father goes down to the pub after dinner. So does Sarah's. We could come after that, about seven. A fire would be great. Sarah would like it, I know."

He could see that she wanted to get away.

"I'll get a big pile of wood, then," he said, walking backward to the edge of the bank. "See you at seven."

VIII

That night, for the first time in a week, Rachel took the path to Sarah's house. The back door screen was latched shut, the verandah unoccupied and in darkness, but at the side of the house, cast on the sand beneath Sarah's window, a golden carpet of light led directly to her room.

Rachel peered in. There was Sarah, still in overalls, curled in her chair reading, and Rachel tapped on the window to attract her attention.

Sarah looked up with a start. The light from the unshaded bulb that dangled, kinked and crooked, from her ceiling fell directly upon the glass, and she saw no more than her own reflection staring steadily back. She could see nothing on the other side.

Rachel tapped again, saying, "Sarah, Sarah," but her voice was caught by the night wind, and when Sarah had uncurled and cupped her hands against the glass to peer through, she laughed to see Rachel there, her mouth opening and closing on silence, like the stupid toadfish that flopped free from the nets onto the jetty. So instead of attempting to speak, she signaled that she would come out, and in no time they were walking through the sandhills toward the ocean beach, laughing and nudging each other from the path into the tufts of gray sea grass that covered the dunes on either side. Right then, there were no words that they could say.

When the dunes were behind them and the silvered sea rollers and wind-driven sands of the beach lay ahead, Rachel stopped and turned. "Sorry, Sarah. Sorry about everything. I don't know what else to say. There are things happening that I can't understand, that I can't keep up with. When Mum died, I thought that I would be all right. I thought that I would be able to work everything out for myself. But I can't. There are things that I can't . . ."

Sarah had stopped too but, having thought of no worthwhile response, walked on. Rachel was forced to catch up to her, protesting, "I'm telling you that I'm sorry, and you walk away."

"Just talk," Sarah said, still walking. "Say what you have to. You know that I've been waiting every day for you to tell me what the matter is."

There was silence; but Sarah was prepared to wait. She knew Rachel well enough. Besides, she would not have cared if Rachel said nothing. She was satisfied to have her back. The night was clear and moonlit, the beach long and deserted. They had time. She bent and picked up a crowned shell from the weed at the tide line and, placing it in the palm of her hand, turned its pearly surface to be lit by the moon. What mattered was that they were back together; there had been a change—something or other had happened, she wasn't sure what—but here they were, all the same. She was satisfied with that.

"I'll tell you something," Rachel said, her voice so soft that Sarah had to turn and walk crabwise to catch her words above the wind. "But don't ask any questions until I'm finished. All right?"

Sarah nodded—it seemed the sensible thing to do—and Rachel began.

"Remember when that boy walked in, wheeling a motorbike. . . ." Sparing no detail, she told of her visits to Sam, from their first meeting until the time she had last seen him, only hours before. Sarah listened as she had been instructed, but when all had been told, or she judged that it had, she dropped the shell from her hand and turned in her tracks. "It's time I got back," she said. "Mum might be worried."

Again Rachel was forced to follow. "Your mum isn't thinking about you and you know it," she said. "You're angry with me, aren't you?"

She grabbed Sarah's arm. "You think that I've left you out."

Sarah was heading for home, walking quickly and deliberately. She felt Rachel's hand on her, pulling her back, but refused to stop.

"It had to happen sometime," she said. "I guess it might as well be now. The funny thing is, I just got my birthday present from you. From that book club. It was there today when I got home. That free book isn't a novel; it's a notebook. It's really nice paper. And I'll use it, don't worry. But I suppose that all the time I was thinking about thanking you, you were down there digging with him. Or whatever it is that the two of you do."

Rachel stopped. From behind she said, "You talk rubbish. You make things up. You imagine things."

Sarah turned. "Do I? Am I imagining that you're going back to him tonight. You are, aren't you?"

They stood face to face on the open beach. The wind off the sea whipped their hair against their faces, across their eyes.

"Sarah," Rachel said, reaching out and putting her hands on her friend's shoulders, "you're wrong. He is nice. He is good-looking. And smart. All of that is true. But . . ."

Sarah laughed. "Who's talking rubbish now?" she said, pulling away.

Rachel sighed. "This is silly. What do you think is going to happen? That I'm going to fall in love and run away with him? Don't be stupid. He's only down here weekends, and he'll be finished with his research in a couple of weeks. Besides, you don't think someone like him—as smart as he is—is going to want to hang around here, do you?"

Sarah said nothing. She was not convinced.

But Rachel had not finished. She looked out over

the sea, as if to prepare. "There's something else. Something queer, and I want you to know because I want you to come back with me now and meet him, and see what you think."

"What? First you tell me how terrific he is, how good-looking and sophisticated and intelligent, and now . . . You're not making sense. . . ."

"You remember last Sunday in church when I was staring up at the fisherman's window and you thought I was having a fit or something? Well, that's part of the trouble. It was like I saw his face in the window."

"Looking in at you?"

"No. No. How could anyone look in the fisherman's window? Don't be . . ."

"I think . . ." Sarah began, but Rachel cut her off.

"Shut up," she said. She was walking again and stepped suddenly ahead and turned to walk backward, to speak more directly.

"It's hard enough to explain as it is. Now, listen. In the folds of the fisherman's robe, or whatever you call it, in the drapery, I was sure that I saw a face. Not the face of one of the women at his feet. Not the ones writing in the book. This was higher, between their heads. And not edged with lead, like the others, but different. Another face that I never saw before. It just appeared . . . out of the material . . . out of nothing, like a vision."

Sarah stopped walking. Her hands went to her head, partly to grab at her wild hair, partly to hold her hands over her ears, showing her disbelief.

"Rachel. Rachel. Rachel," she said. "And you say that *I* imagine things. How could . . ."

But Rachel would not give up and, even in the darkness, Sarah saw that she was in earnest and took her hands from her ears and held her hair from behind.

"I saw this beautiful face, like a woman's face, I thought—dark, not so much the skin, but the eyes—and I knew that I had seen it before, but I couldn't think where, but the blue light from the window glass was falling on me, you see, changing me—my skin—to blue, and now I know that it was like the light in Sam's tent, in his blue plastic tent, you see, and the face in the window was his. I mean the same as his."

Who is this person? Sarah thought. *Is this my Rachel?* "Well," she said, "tomorrow at the service I'll sit in that seat and then I'll see for myself."

Rachel was shaking her head. "No. Come down with me now and meet Sam, and then you can compare and know that I'm not lying. Or mad. Which is what you're thinking, isn't it? Isn't it?"

Sarah did not answer at once. She was looking beyond Rachel, toward the dark ridge of the sand dunes.

"Yes," she said. "I'll come with you, but let's make sure we go alone."

Turning to follow her gaze, Rachel saw the unmistakable white of the Father's robes fluttering on the dunes above them and beside him a darker form, tall and still, which they knew to be the Angel.

Nativity

There was no doubt that Sam had been waiting, hoping that the girls would come. In front of the tent he had built a fire of mangrove roots and dragged others around it, to make a rough circle, "To be friendly," he said when he was introduced.

Rachel picked a log big enough for two and pulled the staring Sarah down beside her while he made billy tea, tipping it into white enamel mugs edged with blue. Rachel did not take one—although he had brought it for her—but Sarah did.

"Mind your lips," he said. "These mugs get hot and burn. The man at the place where I bought the tent told me that they're what campers use, and I didn't know any better. I should have bought plastic."

Rachel said something in agreement. Sarah said

nothing but continued to stare. He took his tea and sat on the other side of the fire. With the distance between them and the wispy gray smoke, Sarah could not see him clearly. Still, she was prepared to sip her tea and wait; to let him and Rachel talk—at least for a while.

So she listened to what he had done after Rachel left that afternoon, and how much more he had to do. When he had finished working at the bank itself, he would move up onto the sand of the clearing to take soundings, as he called them, to check the size of the midden, which extended, as he guessed, from the tea-tree bush right across to the lantana thicket.

At the mention of the lantana, Sarah shuddered. Unnameable fears of childhood stirred in her, and she shifted involuntarily to glance behind, into the blackness beyond the fire. When she turned back and looked across at him, she saw the firelight glint in his eyes and knew that she had been noticed.

"It seems darker back there, doesn't it?" he said. "I don't like that scrub much either. After the first night here, I put my tent up so the opening faced that way. I didn't want that behind me, with its stems creaking and groaning like they do."

"Sorry?" Rachel said, having missed Sarah's look and not knowing what he was talking about. "What's behind you?"

"Nothing," he said. "Shadows. The dark."

Sarah could not resist.

"Is that honestly your name?" she said. "Samuel Shadows?"

At once Rachel's elbow rammed her ribs. "Sarah! That's terrible."

Sam laughed. "It's OK. Sure. That's my name. That's what they told me it was."

"What do you mean, *they* told you? Who? Your mum and dad?"

She leaned forward to shove at a smoldering log as Rachel elbowed air, hissing, "Sarah, shut up."

"I never knew my parents," he said. "People at the boys' home gave me this name."

Sarah would not give up. "But Shadows," she said. "Why call you that?"

He did not answer at once, and save for the licking of flames, and the rumble of surf on the distant bar, the night was silent. Then he said softly, "We all have names, don't we? Someone gave you a name, didn't they?"

"Yes," she began, "but . . ."

"Tell me your name," he said. "Go on."

"That's silly," she said. "Rachel told you that when we were . . ."

"Say it," he said, so that she could not refuse.

"Sarah."

"Sarah what? Go on. Finish it. Sarah what?"

"Goodwin," she said. "This is . . ."

To Rachel he said, "Now say yours. The same. Say it in full."

"Sam . . ." She was confused. She could not understand what was happening.

"No," he corrected. "Not *my* name. *Yours.* Say it. All of it."

"Rachel Burgess."

He laughed, but not his happy-go-lucky laugh that Rachel had liked.

"See? You have names. Both of you. Two full names. And so did your mums and dads and grandmas and grandpas."

"My mother is dead," Rachel said. "And my grandparents. Sarah's are too."

"But you knew them. You saw them. Didn't you? Or pictures of them. I saw nothing. I've got nothing. Not even something I could say belonged to them, to prove that they even lived."

He reached for a log and tossed it on the fire. The sparks spiraled upward, then vanished. "I can tell people now," he said. "That's come with going to the university. I feel more confident now than I did. But there are still things that I need to know.

"I should tell you about the home first, and my room there, because that's what I remember at the beginning. My room had a white iron bed in the corner, and beside it was a cupboard, an old varnished cupboard of dark wood where they kept my clothes.

There was nothing else, no other furniture, only three windows, frosted glass casements with white painted frames that opened parallel, but because the glass was frosted, I couldn't see out, not if I was in the bed; to look out I had to get up and cross the room and stand at a certain angle. Outside was a concreted rectangle of a yard and playground things for kids: a concrete pipe painted green that was never painted fresh in my time, and a red slippery slide and yellow swings, all streaked with rust. Around the yard was a high wire fence, and beyond the fence was a bitumen lane and a brick wall. They're my first memories, and now it's hard to keep them separate, to stop them from getting confused with what came later, such as the desk, which I didn't get until I went to high school.

"This place was called the Home, and I lived there all my life, right up until I went to the university and moved into the residential college on campus. But that was only recently, only the other day in the terms of this story, so don't judge anything I say from that angle. I mean, from the point of view of my being a university student, because that would be false. It wasn't until I was in high school that I even thought to read the writing on the sign outside the home, although I walked past it every day. It said, 'The Lia Damalla Home for Boys.' Then in the smallest printing, which was faded and peeling, it said, 'A Division of the State Children's Services,' and there was a phone number.

"There were usually ten or twelve kids in the home. They didn't have their own rooms like me. I was lucky. They shared, two or three to a room. It was a long time later that I found out the reason that I had a room to myself. And I can show you, right now . . ."

He reached into his back pocket and withdrew a wallet, opened it, and half-standing, handed a photograph across the fire to Rachel.

For a moment Sarah saw his face, lit from beneath by the low flames. *Yes*, she thought, *he is what Rachel said. Only better.*

Then he sat down and was speaking again. "She might look like my grandmother," he said, "but she's more of a fairy godmother. She was the one who looked after me there. She got me my own room."

Sarah looked at the photo in Rachel's hand. There was nothing remarkable in the face that she saw: a woman of about seventy, her gray hair drawn back, her mouth and jaw set, although her eyes were soft.

"That's Mrs. Hibbert," he said. "The home boys just called her Hibbert. She didn't mind. She was the supervisor of the home from the time I can first remember until I was sixteen. She was always good to me, and like I said, she was the one who got me my room and a stack of other things. She was the one who gave me my name."

He took something else from his wallet, a square of folded paper. A letter.

"It's all here, but I'll tell you something more important first, because like I said, there are still things that I need to know—and I hope that you can help me."

Rachel handed the photo back. "What things?" she said.

"Sorry. You don't know what I'm talking about. Well, from here on, it gets easier. Hibbert looked after me from the beginning. I had no family and no visitors. Some of the other kids would go back home, or move out, or get fostered or adopted. But I didn't. If I said anything to Hibbert, like asked her questions about who I was or how come I was in the home, she would give me these vague answers, like 'You're mine,' or 'That's a long story,' and then she would tickle me or chase me or hug me or some other thing to get my mind off what I asked. Even later, when I was in high school and really wanted to know and asked the sort of questions you did, Sarah, about my name, she still wouldn't tell. At least not much. One time she said, 'You came in without papers' and another time, when I really pushed her because kids at school were laughing at me about my name, she said, 'I gave you that name, and be grateful you've got one.' So she wasn't any help and I gave up trying. She was there and the home and everything went on day after day. You know, nothing changed.

"Then, when I was starting my last year of high school and was looking forward to being a senior, she came to me one night after dinner and said that she needed to talk to me. She had done that before, if something was important. 'Here?' I said, but she shook her head and took me into her little office off the hallway. I thought that she was going to tell me something about school, like I couldn't go or something. I knew that she'd had trouble getting me enrolled to do my final year. The bureaucrats at the State Children's Services had already tried to stop me from going on. I was supposed to leave and find a job when I was fifteen. It was Hibbert who helped me through that mess. So I was ready to hear that the squabble was on again, but she said, 'Sam, they have got me at last. I'm sixty-six. I should have retired last year. Now they are making me go. I have to be out in a week.'

"When the staff and the boys were lined up in the hallway to say good-bye to her and my turn came, she gave someone the bunch of flowers she was holding and pulled me close and hugged me. I was crying by then, and that started her off too, but she said, 'Don't look back. Always look ahead.' And that's exactly what she did herself. She walked straight down the hall and out the door. The person with the flowers went after her, and she took them, then next thing she was in a cab and gone.

"When Hibbert left, the department sent in what was called the new order. We didn't have one supervisor like her anymore, acting like a mother. The department sent in these young social workers, mostly males, and they spent their time arranging outings and games and being our 'buddies.' That was the 'in' word, *buddies*. The little kids thought this was terrific. For the first time the concrete playground outside my window was filled with kids running around yelling and screaming. I was allocated a 'buddy' too. He was twenty-one. He hadn't been out of the university for long. His name was John Jordan, but he said to call him Jordy. He was OK, but at the age I was then, nearly seventeen, and with the schoolwork that I had to do, I didn't really need some guy trying to entertain me. Besides, if I had wanted a buddy, there were plenty of kids my own age at school that I could hang around with. As it turned out, I had trouble working out what to talk to Jordy about, how to make him feel useful. Then at Easter of that year, the kids in my class who were intending to take their final exams were asked to fill in these preliminary forms for examination nomination, and there were certain questions that I couldn't answer. The next time Jordy came around to my room, I asked him if he could help. That was the first time I had asked him for anything, and he was happy. I told him about the questions on the form, and he said, 'What sort of questions exactly?' so I showed him: nationality of parents, place of birth. Things like that. He was sitting on the desk that Hibbert had got for me when I started high school. It was under the windows that I mentioned before, looking out over the playground. When I told him that I didn't know this information, he looked at me; then when he should have said something, he looked away out of the windows.

"I thought, *What's the matter with this guy? For months he hangs around wanting to help, then when I ask for it, he ignores me.* I said, 'So what am I supposed to do?' He turned back to me then. 'How long have you been looking at this view?' he said, and I told him. 'All my life, that I can remember.' 'What about your family?' he said. 'Your mum or dad. Which one of them put you here?' I told him that I didn't know and didn't have anyone. He shook his head and got up and left. I thought, *What the hell use is he?* and chucked the form to one side and got on with my homework. I thought I would go and see my school principal and ask him what to do.

"Then, a couple of minutes later, Jordy came back. He said he wanted to talk to me, and I got up and sat on my bed so that he could sit on my desk chair, but he didn't. He shifted the books and perched on the corner of the desk. 'Do you like studying?' he said. I told him that I didn't especially, but it helped pass the time, and if I didn't look after myself, nobody else would. Then he said, 'What job would you like?' I told him that I didn't know, that I hadn't even thought about it, but probably outside work, and that I wanted a piece of paper with what I was printed on it. My title and qualifications. I wanted to be someone. He said, 'Would you like to come out to the university with me one day? To have a look around?' I was starting my final year of high school, so I thought that would be OK.

"Then he said, 'There's something that I want to tell you.' He looked me straight in the eye. 'I found out something about you. Some information about your mother.' I didn't say anything. 'There is a file on you here. They have had information on you from the beginning, filed in the supervisor's office. By law, it's your right to see the file. I can get it for you now and leave it with you, or you might like me to stay, and we could go through it together. It's your choice.'

"I said, 'Have you looked?' and he nodded. I said, 'Do you think you should stay?' He nodded again. He said he thought it would be best but he would leave any time if I asked. I said that it would be OK if he stayed, and waited in the room while he went down the hall to the office to get the file.

"I remember sitting on my bed waiting and wondering what I would know, and what he knew, and what gave anyone the right to know anything about myself that I didn't know already, or choose to tell, maybe.

"When he came back, he had an ordinary manila folder. 'This is your file,' he said. 'Do you want to look

at it over there, or here?' He was on the desk again,
but this time I got up and sat next to him. I could see
my name printed on a file tab at the top of the folder.
He held it out to me. 'I found this the day I was allocated to you as a buddy. The file was where it should
have been, in the office filing cabinet, in correct alpha-
betical order by surname. It's no longer legal to with-
hold information, although it's not unusual for it to
happen, especially in places like this.'

"I opened the folder and right away saw a form
with personal details. Where it said 'Father's Name'
there was nothing but an empty space, but where it
said 'Mother's Name' there was a name, Hannah, and
after that the letters *O.N.O.* I said, 'What does that
mean?' 'One Name Only,' Jordy said, 'which means
that Hannah, who was your mother, had no other
name, no middle name, and no known surname.' I
said, 'Why would that be?' and he shook his head and
tapped the folder for me to go on. No matter what
was supposed to be on that form, it didn't appear: no
residential address for this Hannah, no details of her
employment or family background. I thought this was
a waste of time and said so.

"Beneath that form there were others: my medical
history, my school reports, but not much else. Nothing
personal about who I was. I could feel tears starting,
and Jordy said, 'There's this as well,' and he flicked
over to the back of the file, where there was an enve-

lope. He said, 'I admit that I read this, but I think it is your business only, and I don't believe it should be in that file anymore. Maybe it should never have been.'"

Sam held up the folded letter that he had taken from his wallet. "This was in that envelope," he said. "You might as well hear the real thing. It's all that I know about me. How I got my name. Everything. And it's what brought me down here. And why I need your help. It's a letter, written by Hibbert. One of you can read it if you want to. I'll make another lot of tea."

"I will," Sarah said, reaching out. But when she took the letter from him and unfolded it, she muttered, "I can't read this. It's all written by hand. And there's no light."

"Hang on," he said. "I'll get the lamp."

He put the billycan back on the fire, then unhooked the lamp from the center post of his tent. Kneeling in the sand, he primed and lit it, and when the light was full and steady, he held it out to Sarah, still watching from the other side of the fire.

"Where?" he asked.

"There," she said, indicating where he stood. "Put it on the sand. I'll come around."

He did as she said, but as she moved to his side, to sit on his log outside the tent, he turned at once to where she had been and took her position next to Rachel.

He grinned. "A bit like musical chairs, isn't it?"

Sarah saw his arm disappear behind Rachel, as if to steady himself, and since their eyes were on her, waiting, Sarah was left with no option but to read.

"To future staff of the Lia Damalla Home: Confidential. Re: the boy known as Samuel Shadows.

"As I have been informed that I must retire from my position as supervisor of this institution, and since I am the last of those who know the full history of the above-mentioned boy and his parentage—insofar as he might be said to have a history, or, for that matter, a parentage—I record these details for future reference, but let the reader take note: should any of the information recorded here be made known to the boy, or otherwise allowed to fall into his hands, then that person shall bear full responsibility for the outcome, and the damage [or otherwise] to his welfare which may ensue.

"This home, now reserved for the exclusive use of boys in compromising social circumstances, has served two previous occupancies. The first was that of its original owner—and later his heirs—who cut the property from the virgin bush and built the residence, calling it Lia Damalla, the name, as the story goes, being chosen by the wife, and derived from the local Aboriginal word for 'nest' or 'shelter.' However, following a considerable decline in fortune, during what is now referred to as the Great Depression, these persons were forced to offer their residence for sale, and by virtue of its solid structure and exceptional size, it was considered appropriate by certain officers of the government to purchase the property for use as a retreat for wayward women, as certain girls, unfortunate enough to discover themselves with child, were called at that time.

"It was during the latter stages of this second occupancy that I took up office as matron of the Lia Damalla Retreat, and in that time the girl, Hannah, soon to give birth to the boy known today as Samuel Shadows, came into my care.

"On the night of Hannah's arrival, my girls [as I preferred to call them] had only just finished hearing grace, prior to commencing their evening meal, when there was a knock at the front door. There stood two police officers, both of whom were known to me, as they had brought young women for admission on previous occasions, and supported between them was a girl on the verge of collapse.

"They brought her in at once, and by the hallway lamps I saw that she was dark, of mixed race, probably European and Aboriginal, although from the shape of her face, which was fine featured and quite lovely, she could have been of Island descent, possibly Melanesian. But above all other considerations was her age; she was a slip of a thing, no more than fifteen years old, I imagined.

"Seeing no bag or other personal belongings, I said, 'Has she any things? Any identification?' But the officers shook their heads, and one said, 'We found her in a park. People heard her in the bushes. We got her out, but she told us nothing, and she's got nothing, so we brought her here.'

"Indicating the reception chair beside the hallstand, I left to get help, but when I returned with one of my assistants, not two minutes later, both officers were gone, no doubt considering their duty done, and the girl sat by herself, almost lost from sight among the dim shadows of the hall. 'She's no more than a shadow herself,' my assistant remarked, having noted the girl's color and her frailty, and that word, *Shadows*, became her name, since she offered no other, save her Christian name, which she told us was Hannah.

"So the girl known as Hannah Shadows came to stay with us, but it was some time before we realized her true condition, that she was pregnant, and that her baby was most likely due in a matter of four or five months.

"When Hannah's son was born, there was not a woman in the hostel who did not remark upon his beauty, and be assured, there had been many beautiful children born in that place. Certainly the shape of his head and the features of his face were perfect, and likewise his eyes—being exceptionally dark—were another of his mother's legacies. But not his skin, which was fairer by far than his mother's and led us all to believe that his father had been white.

"Three days after the birth—which took place in the very room that the boy occupies to this day—I approached the mother again in what had become a futile effort to discover any details of her personal background and family. I was obliged to learn all I could in order that arrangements might be made for her safe return home following the period of her confinement, or, failing this, the adoption of the baby so that she might be free to find work.

"Once more my efforts were in vain. At first I had believed the girl to be hard and canny, of the type who will, on principle, deny information to any authority, considering such communication to be synonymous with human weakness and a shame. I had learned nothing from her, other than her Christian name, which I have already said to be Hannah. Nor would she engage in conversation sufficient even to name her own child—and this was not because she paid it no attention—indeed she held it to herself as it if were the only thing she might call her own, in this life or any other, a sad fact which was to prove true enough. Eventually, after due consideration, the remainder of the staff agreed to call the baby Samuel, since a child bearing that name in Holy Scripture had a mother called Hannah, and he had lived to become a great man, of extraordinary spirit.

"As the child grew, there was considerable discussion among the staff of what gainful work Hannah might undertake. To all, one thing was obvious: irrespective of where she had come from, the girl was not ready to return to the outside world, either to seek work or otherwise to fend for herself. Having carefully observed her behavior and, in particular, her obvious love and care for the child, we concluded that she was all that she appeared and that in her simple and childlike manner there was no artifice, rather, she was utterly naïve and ignorant of all but the most elementary forms of social intercourse. So it came about that Hannah Shadows began work in the retreat as a general domestic, a role she carried out as though she had performed such menial duties all her life. And while she did eventually speak—though only when necessary, and never of herself or her past—she lived as her name implies, always on the edge of things, as if she were constantly afraid.

"The Lord, however, works in mysterious ways. After some months of service it was noted by many that Hannah was not herself and that, although she had always been thin, she now appeared wan and drawn and lacked even the stamina to manage her daily round of duties, let alone care for her baby. For some days she lay in her bed, refusing food, and denying all offers of assistance, and when the seriousness of her condition became apparent, she was admitted to a hospital; but no doctor could diagnose the nature of her illness.

"In my time I have seen several of my girls die, but never did I see one slip away as quickly as Hannah Shadows. Either a member of my staff, or myself, maintained a constant watch by her bedside, but she continued to refuse sustenance, and to all appearances gradually lost the will to live. When her condition became so low that it was certain she would leave us, a priest was called to administer to her needs; and if I had not been at her side at this time, I would not have believed what I now record.

"The priest was a young man, in residence at the hospital, and pleasant and appealing—in no way intimidating in his simple surplice of white linen—but no sooner had he knelt beside her, so that her eyes might focus on him and understand his intention, than the girl turned away in a burst of energy that amazed us, and presuming that she was filled with terror at the prospect of death, he put his hand upon her shoulder, exposed before him, about to cleanse her soul of some dreadful misdemeanor, but at his touch there came from the girl's mouth a stream of invective and vile language that would better suit the devil himself, and the priest, realizing to his horror that this attack was directed at him, turned to me for explanation. I had none to offer.

"When he had gone, I knelt by her bed, taking her

hand, but she would not look at me, though her grasp grew tighter. 'Hannah,' I said, 'you must tell me. What could be so terrible that it can't be told to me? I have cared for you from the beginning. I delivered your baby.'

"At the mention of the child, she looked up and spoke at last. 'Will I die?' she said. Since I could not answer her, she knew at once what I was certain of. 'You keep my baby,' she said. 'You keep him safe. I know the color of his skin. Let him be white. None of us blacks are left. Not in New Canaan. There is none left. Soon, nowhere.' I swear that those were the words she said, and after them she did not speak again—at least, not in a language that could be reckoned intelligible—and in a matter of hours, she died.

"This was the reason that I kept her boy, and some years later, when the Good Lord exercised His Will and the retreat became the home that it is today, I was appointed as the supervisor. Since he was already living at the home, Samuel Shadows became the first of my boys and has remained the first in my heart ever since.

"Now I am no longer permitted to hold this position. There are regulations which state that at my age I must retire. I believe that it is well known that I have several times attempted to adopt Samuel Shadows as my own. These efforts have been in vain. I am told that as a single woman it is not expedient for me to raise a child; or, more often of late, they tell me that I am too old.

"In my life of service I have known many mothers, held many children, and I am yet to find that person, of any age, sex, race, or creed, who has no need for love.

"The boy knows nothing of the contents of his file, or of this document. As I have said, should they be made known to him, then such knowledge is against the wishes of his mother, and the responsibility for the outcome will not be mine.

"Elizabeth Hibbert, supervisor, the Lia Damalla Home for Boys."

Sarah finished reading and looked up. "New Canaan," she said. "It says so right here. You might have come from here."

"I might." He nodded. "But it also says that I'm black, doesn't it? Like my mother."

"So?" Rachel said, half-turning to him.

"I'm black. That's what it says. That I'm not like you."

The fire crackled over their silence.

Sarah folded the letter. When he reached out to take it, she said, "If you cut that hand, you know, opened a vein or something in your wrist, you would bleed red blood, wouldn't you? Like me and Rachel?"

He looked away, into the dark.

"But wouldn't you?" she said.

"You know I would."

Rachel broke the silence. "Well, that's that. But what I want to know is: did you ever see Hibbert again, to find out more?" She grabbed his arm above the elbow and shook him until he grinned.

"That's better. Well? Did you?"

"Sure. Jordy took me. He knew where she lived. She had this weatherboard place out in the suburbs. Jordy phoned her and said that we would be coming, and when we got there, she was all ready, and we had afternoon tea. Halfway through cutting the cake she put the knife down and came around the table and hugged me, saying that I was her boy. And all that."

He laughed. "I was happy then, because I knew that there was someone.

"She asked me if I would leave the home and come live with her. I said that when I left school I wanted to have a go at living by myself, but that I would come around and see her once a week and mow her yard and anything else she wanted. Then I couldn't pretend anymore and told her straight out that I knew about the file and my mother. She wasn't happy. She blamed Jordy for telling me and would have sent him packing, but I told her it was all right, that I was glad that I knew, and after that she calmed down. I asked her to tell me all she could about my mother, what she looked like and things like that, and she told me some stories—just episodes in the home—and described my mother for me, which was great, but there was nothing else she could add about her other life or her family—my family—and I was sure then that I would never know. And when it was time to go, we got down to the gate and Hibbert said, 'Do you like this house?' I said that I did—which was true—and she laughed and said, 'That's good, because when I'm gone, it's yours.' She said, 'I'm like you. I haven't got anyone either. And even if you had never come around, it was yours. I had a solicitor do up a will.' I didn't know what to say. Here I was with her again, and she was already talking about dying."

"But what about here?" Rachel said. "Did she say more about New Canaan?"

"No. Nothing. But there were a couple of things that I knew for sure—my mother's name, Hannah, that she was most likely black, part Aboriginal, Hibbert said, and that this place, New Canaan, had something to do with me. And I wasn't going to forget any of that. Jordy said he would come down here, since it would have to be where my mother came from. Hibbert said my mother wasn't tough enough to be a city girl.

"So he came and asked around if anyone knew this Hannah. There was no one who did. Besides, we never did find out her real surname, and there were no Aborigines around here and hadn't been for years.

He stayed overnight in that pub, the Fisherman's Rest, but he found out nothing. He said no one would answer his questions; everyone just stood there and shook their heads. It was all a waste of time. I guess the fishermen thought he was crazy, coming looking for some black girl who might have lived here nearly twenty years ago. And he went to the priest, the one you call Gray Eye, I guess, and he knew nothing either. Or wouldn't tell him if he did. And Rachel, that's how come I asked you about the Father, how long he had been here and all that. But when Jordy came back and told me, I said to drop it. What was the point? Even if I had relations, they didn't know who I was. They didn't even know that I was born.

"I was getting ready for my final exams then, and I worked harder than ever before—maybe it was to pretend that nothing was wrong—but by the end of that year, I had good results and made up my mind about what I wanted to do. I wanted to do this degree in anthropology. And maybe learn something about how my people lived and the place they lived in once, if I could find that country."

He reached down for another log and tossed it onto the seething heart of the fire.

"Well," Sarah said. "Go on."

"I read in the university handbook how there was a combined degree in anthropology and archaeology, and how graduates were in demand to research ancient tribal sites and sacred places endangered by mining or agriculture. I thought that would be what I wanted. I would be outside, and have a degree, and be someone."

Sam watched the flames flare around the green wood.

"So that's what I did. I got out of the home and spent some time with Hibbert. I stayed at her place until university started. That was last Christmas, and it was the best. On Christmas day Jordy came over, and there we were, the three of us. It was the first time I felt like I was part of a family. Then after Christmas dinner the two of them up and disappeared, and there I was with all the dishes, and the next thing I hear them calling me from the backyard, and I looked out the kitchen window, and they were outside her garden shed with this amazing bike—my motorbike—that one."

He nodded toward the machine standing beside the tent. "Hibbert had put up the money, and Jordy had gone out and chosen it. I didn't even have a license.

"When I started at the university, I liked the life on campus straight away; the courses that I picked, and being away from the little kids at the home. And when my anthropology lecturer set our major assignment, I already knew what I wanted to do. One of my tutors had given us a research exercise on the locality and composition of shell middens. It was just a minor thing to get us used to using the reference texts in the library, but when I was getting material for that, I came across this book that was written in 1900, and in a footnote I saw the name New Canaan. It said that one of the largest oyster middens on the East Coast was beside the New Canaan lagoon, and that the size of the midden indicated that the local Aboriginal population had been between a hundred and a hundred and fifty people, which suggested a very important and prosperous tribe. But by the time the midden had been noted and recorded by Europeans, there were only twenty or thirty of these people remaining in the lagoon area. So I thought, *This is something. I can follow this up and find a tribal name and read about someone who might be mine—or from my country at least.* But there was nothing else. Not anywhere. I found other books that mentioned this place, but they always said the same thing: 'There is an oyster midden at New Canaan.' Nothing about the tribe that put it there, or the tribe's name, or how come there weren't any Aborigines near the place anymore. I started to wonder if somehow each writer had copied the other's material, and maybe the story had grown from there—maybe the whole midden story was false—a scientific hoax. As if the coastal tribes never existed.

"That was early this year, and the research I did got me interested in trying to find anything I could about local Aborigines—I mean tribes that occupied country within a hundred miles of the city, along the coast, and inland too—but in every case there was nothing. Since I was living on campus, I didn't see so much of Jordy but he told me about urban Aboriginal groups that had 'get-togethers,' and I went to some. The people were all right, friendly, and there were plenty of others that had pale skin like mine. Some people listened if I asked about the tribes from down this way, but most said what Jordy had already told me: that there had been no Murries—that's the name they called themselves—living down New Canaan way for years. And even the older ones, who said that they had known the Canaan mob—they didn't know a proper tribal name for them either—they said that there had only been a few living there and they had disappeared years ago. That's all I heard, and after a while I decided that going to the get-togethers was not so good for me. Not at that time anyway. The others all had relations there, and everyone seemed to know who they were. I still knew nobody, and next to nothing about myself.

"That was when I decided about the big assignment; to get organized and come down here, to find out what I could for myself. I figured that even if I came to a dead end about my mother and her people, at least I would be able to see the country where they might have lived. If they even existed."

There was a long silence, and Sam looked up from

the coals to see both girls looking at him—Rachel beside him, Sarah opposite—both searching his face, almost in fear.

"Ooops," he said and dropped his head into his hands to hide his embarrassment. "I did it again, didn't I, Rachel? You should never let me get going. Sorry."

Rachel laughed and pushed him with her fist. "Don't worry. You should be around when Sarah gets going. She gets more wound up than you . . . and what's worse, she makes half of her stories up."

"Lovely," Sarah said. "Charming. Why not say that your best friend's got a big mouth? Besides, it was you who spun the story that got me down here, remember?"

"What?" Sam said. "What's going on?"

"Nothing." This was Rachel, trying her best to catch Sarah's eye across the glow of the fire. But she was wasting her time.

"There is something," Sarah said. "And Rachel won't tell you, I know. Down at the church there's a stained glass window, and she says your face is in it. The shape of your face. That's what I was talking about."

"Sarah!" Rachel was on her feet, and Sam reached up, pulling her back, still protesting, beside him.

"My face in stained glass? Hibbert would love that. Am I up there with the saints? Are there angels flapping all around me? This I have to see!"

But Rachel was not going to sit still and be made fun

of. As soon as Sam relaxed his grip, she was up again, and before he could stop her, she had stepped around the fire to Sarah and stood above her, scowling.

"You had to tell him, didn't you? It might surprise you to know that I was thinking about the church, but not the window. I was thinking about the great book. See? Old Gray Eye's great book, and what might be recorded in it. Now do you see? Now do you get it?"

Sarah understood at once. "Sam's mother," she said. "She might be in it. If she came from here. The Father must know."

She got up and faced the confused Sam. "We're not crazy. We're just thinking aloud. It's all right to do that if you're nearly twins, which we are. Down at the church the Father keeps this book. The locals call it his great book. A register of all that's happened here—births, deaths, marriages, accidents . . ."

"So they say," Rachel added. "We haven't seen it . . ."

"But our mothers have. When they cleaned his place, where he lives, behind the church. I heard them . . ."

"Wait," he said, raising both hands in the air. "Hold everything. It's like I'm listening to you in stereo. Just wait. First there's a window, and then there's a book. What am I supposed to believe? Tell me."

"I guess that I started this," Rachel said, "so I better tell it," and patting the log to indicate that he should sit, she told him about the blue light and the face in the window.

"But it's nothing," she said. "I'm sure now that it was all in my head. Just a mind game. I was probably upset by something else."

She did not mention the trouble with Angel, and Sarah respected that, saying nothing.

"But what about this book that your friend Gray Eye keeps?"

"He isn't our friend, and never has been. He doesn't trust us at all. But I think that there's a book. He's supposed to record everything. He's that sort, isn't he, Sarah? Strange."

Sarah nodded. She was satisfied now. Not only had Rachel apologized—in a way—but while she had been speaking, Sarah had picked up the lamp, quite naturally since it was in danger of being kicked, and holding it high, had seen Sam's face. She looked at him carefully. The words in Hibbert's letter were very clear: "the features . . . perfect, and likewise his eyes . . . exceptionally dark . . ." Sarah laughed to herself; no wonder Hibbert loved him. And maybe Rachel too . . . but she wouldn't think about that, not now.

"I reckon there's a book," she said. "But whether it's some special book, as they say, or whether it's just a birth and death register, who knows? But I'm sure there is one. And that's a start, Sam. Ask the Father yourself."

"Tomorrow is Sunday. We could come down and get you and take you," Rachel said.

"Yes. We could come down after . . ." Sarah hesitated, not willing to say "after the service of women." "We could come down after lunch."

Watchers by Night

I

When the girls had gone, Sam covered what remained of the fire and slipped into the tent. But he could not settle, not after what he had been through, after the night's revelations.

What's the point of lying around in here? he asked himself. *I'm never going to sleep.* And getting hold of his sleeping bag, he dragged it out and spread it on the cushioning sand before the tent. Then he lay down, his hands under his head, and looked up at the heavens.

That was a silver night, the night wind drifting fresh across the lagoon, and the stars clear. Yet from where he lay, low down, his line of vision equal to the horizon, there was no way of knowing where earth ended and heaven began, and except that he lay directly above the covered embers of the fire, so that their warmth throbbed beneath him, he might have been anywhere, suspended between heaven and earth.

It's like I can feel the heart of the earth, he thought. *Like the heart of the earth is telling me that it's there.*

And when he had thought a little more, he said out loud, to the silence and the stillness of the night: "So where are you, God the Father? Are you out there on your throne beyond the moon and stars and all the planets, shining in glory unapproachable? And even though you are so great and your power drives the universe, is it true that you can see me here, as you see the birds in their nests, and the fish in their caves in the sea?

"What am I to believe?

"Beneath me I feel a strength that is your equal, yet not so cold; a closer, warmer god of earth. A woman even? A woman bedded-down deep in coals of fire? And is she the one who is mine, with her warmth and closeness here beneath me, and not you, way off among those white and distant stars?"

Then with a sigh he said, "Will you show me? Either one? Will you show me which is mine?"

And out of the lantana, from what had been the edge or outline of night, a shape lifted clear, framed against the pale light of the stars.

It was the Angel who appeared, and stood above him.

"Who is that?" Sam said, not daring to get up. The Angel turned, so that the moon struck his face, silvering the angle of his jaw, the length of his arm, catching on the knuckles and protrusion of veins at the back of his hand. He towered above Sam.

"That bike yours?" he said.

"What?" Sam said, raising himself and arching his neck to look up and back. "Who the hell are you?"

He was alert now. He was down, and whoever this was had the advantage both in position and build. He had come through too many years at the home to show fear.

"Tell me who you are," he said, "or bugger off."

But the Angel stepped forward, his left arm fully visible, and the tautness of its sinew was evident.

"That bike yours?" he said.

From his hand came the flash of a blade and the sound of tearing. He had slashed the tent.

Sam leapt up and stumbled forward, but the flash came again, this time higher, level with his face, and he stopped, aware of the size of his assailant.

"Tell me who you are, and I'll answer your bloody question."

There was no answer. With Angel against the moon Sam could make out nothing, no more than a black mass silhouetted against the light, and he stepped away, to see from the side. Then he felt the push against his chest. Not violent, not sudden or painful, but powerful enough to threaten. At once his blood was up. Slashing the tent was one thing, but touching him was another, and he pushed back, shoving both his hands against the intruder's chest.

"I told you once. Now bugger off."

The Angel laughed. He was enjoying himself. He stepped back, just enough to keep his balance.

"No," he said into Sam's face. "I reckon it's you who should be telling me who you are. I live here, see. It's you who is the outsider. It's you who comes riding in here with your flash bike, hey. Or maybe I should say, walking in here with your flash bike. Because that's what you do. You walk in here so we can all see just how nice your bike is. And hey, I watched you. Just like you wanted me to. And I said to myself, *Angel, you could do with a bike like that. That's a nice bike. Big and red and all shined up. With a bike like that, you could do anything. Go anywhere, and there wouldn't be a woman who would say no.* That's what I said to myself when I seen that bike."

As he spoke, they moved, circling slowly, but all the while Sam distanced himself so that, when the talking had finished, the tent was between them and it was Sam with the moon behind him, and what was visible of the Angel, his head and face, his shoulders and chest, was silvered with moonlight.

Sam said, "Listen, whatever your name is, I don't know what this is about. I don't understand any of that about my bike. I don't know what you think I'm here for, but I didn't come here to make trouble. I'm doing an assignment. I'm doing research for my university course. That's all. So how about you . . ."

They stopped circling, and stood, eyeing each other. The face of the Angel was terrible, the moon squaring the bones of his cheeks and his jaw and hardening the lines of his mouth, setting his grin. He stroked the blade in his hand.

"Don't give me any of your smart-mouth crap. Don't give me any university crap."

He twisted the knife, and the blade flashed a ray of silver into Sam's eyes, so that he turned away, dazzled.

"See. Can't take the truth test, hey? Can't face the light of truth. Don't give me that university bloody crap. I know more. You had girls here last night, hey."

The blade found the light and flashed again.

"You're full of it, bike boy. You don't need to answer. I seen those girls here. I seen them on the beach at sundown, talking like they do—close together and whispering, the same as their mothers used to—then I seen them come the way down here and sit by your fire. Cozy, hey. And you with all that work, all that university work, all that research. Funny how you don't have no job, but you can have a bike like that— that costs that much—and girls too. But me, the working boy—I've got nothing. No girl. No bike. Maybe I should try this university crap—or maybe you're thinking that I'm too dumb, hey? Too stupid."

He reached out, and again there was the sound of tearing.

Sam was afraid now. It was one thing to defend himself, to fight with his hands—he had done that before, and often—but this was different, this was dangerous; these were issues that could not be read, issues deeper than any physical contact could resolve. And worse, he was afraid that his fear would show. It was better to back off.

"Sorry," he said. "Sorry about coming down and upsetting things. I didn't mean to do that. That's how come I walked the bike, not to disturb anyone, and out here I thought I would be alone. Sorry about all this. I won't need to be here much longer. Maybe two or three weekends. No more. Then I should be done. OK?"

But it could not be so simple, and the Angel was smart.

"Sure," he said. "In two weeks, maybe three, you're going to say, 'See ya. So long,' and get on your shiny bike and ride right out of here. Just like that. You must think I'm bloody thick. You think because I'm a local, and not some smart-arse university tight-jean bike boy from the city like yourself, that I don't know the quality of the goods you're handling. The . . ."

"The what?" Sam said. "The quality of the what?"

"The goods. My goods. Not yours. She always was

my girl. The Father told me that from the beginning. From the very start he promised her to me. He named her. He named her straight out. 'I'll keep her for you,' he said. 'I'll give her to you.' I know the quality of the goods. And what's owing to me. So don't you come around here with your city talk and your bike, thinking you're getting her. Thinking that you're going to change anything. It's all decided. It's in the Father's book. In the great book. Me and her. Right there. Like everything else. And you be careful, since I might take a look and see if you're in there too. Like the others. Like the Steele boys, or her mother, that Eva Burgess. They're all dead, hey. And they were in that book. The Father told me. And I seen what happened to them. The net come down for them. So be careful that the Father doesn't come looking out for you."

There was spit about his mouth, silvered on his lips. *He's crazy,* thought Sam. *Out of his head.*

"But even if I don't get the Father and even if he doesn't name you, that don't mean you go walking out. No. Don't you think that . . ."

Once more his hand moved to the sound of tearing.

"You sure this tent is OK? Is it rotten or what?"

"There was a girl here," Sam said. "But I don't see what she's got to do with you, with you coming around like this. Coming around and slashing . . ." and he indicated the tent with his hand.

"Then *you* must be the stupid one," the Angel said,

"since I just told you plain enough. This girl was Rachel Burgess, hey?"

"Sure. Rachel was here."

The Angel came forward, moving around the tent until there was nothing between them. He bent a little to breathe into Sam's face. "So I'm saying that she's mine. See. So get out. That's what you have to do. Get out . . . or . . ."

The blade slashed. Then Sam moved, his arms locked around the Angel's chest, his head butted against him, and with the suddenness the Angel stumbled backward, his foot catching the tent rope, and went down with Sam upon him, straddling him.

"You get out," Sam was saying, "you get out," all the while struggling to pin the Angel's arms beneath his knees and grip the wrist below the glittering blade. But he could not do it.

Once only the Angel brought his fist up under Sam's chin, and Sam, by far the lighter of the two, sprawled backward on the sand, the blood already in his mouth, and in seconds the Angel was on him—the knife quivering at his neck, but then came a moment of stillness, and it seemed to Sam in his pain and fear that another form appeared, white, ghostly, a deathly face, or mask, or skull, stared into his own. Then the knife was gone and the skull face, and there was only the Angel, leering at him, saying, "If I see you with her again, I'll kill you. You got that? You got that good and clear?"

Then he was gone, and Sam lay gasping on the bloodied sand.

II

When morning came, gray at first, then pink, then gold, flooding the lagoon and bathing him in light, Sam said to himself, *Since a messenger has been sent to me, to tell me I'm not wanted, then maybe it's time I met these people on their own ground and let them know that, whatever else happens, I'm not leaving here until I get done what I came to do, until I find out what I want to know, and all the angels of heaven coming around carving things up with knives won't stop me from doing that.*

He undressed, tossing his clothes into what remained of the tent, and dropped over the edge of the bank to wade out through the shallows. Beyond the mangrove stumps where the muddy bottom fell away to become the bar channel, he dived in, immersing himself, allowing the hurt and confusion of the night to wash away until he burst to the surface, shaking his dark, wet hair about his face. He swam easily then, taking his time, but all the while heading for the tumble of rocks that formed the northern bank of the lagoon. As he swam, he felt the strength of the current tugging beneath him, and he knew that if he wanted, he could roll on his back and float, letting the current carry him to the breakers that dumped on the sandbanks of the bar. But he kicked more strongly and increased his stroke until he reached the other side, emerging to sprawl, naked and dripping, on the black slabs of the tumbled rocks.

When the sun had warmed and dried him, he turned his back to the sea and looked back inland, across the lagoon to the jetties, the shabby boatsheds, his own blue tent, and his bike, glinting in the sun. Behind them, blocking any further view of the hinterland, was the gray-green barrier of the tea-tree bush. It was strange, he thought, since beyond that lay New Canaan, less a town than another country. Complete in itself, hidden. Except, of course, for the church, the gleaming needle of its spire protruding from the bush.

Then he sat up, leaning forward to look again. If he broadened his vision, took a wider view, there, beyond the church spire, the towering mass of the core burst from the earth to impale the sky.

III

Sarah wriggled in her pew.

"Where's this face?" she whispered. "I can't see any face."

But when Rachel turned to glare at her, she sat still and, ignoring the ranting of the Father at the altar, stared once again at the robes of the fisherman in the window above her.

The Father was in full flight: "And there shall come a time when your faith in the Lord will be sorely tested, and you will doubt Him, and question Him in your hearts, even turning aside from the paths of your daily life, and saying one to another, 'Who is this One, this Father, who has begotten us? Who is this One, this Father, that He should have power over us? And in the time of need, will He be there when we call?' And will He indeed? For there are those who have said, 'Where was He when the *Seeker* went down, and Aaron Steele was taken, and his sons, caught up in the net? And where was He when Eva Burgess was struck, pierced by the serpent, lying secret even as she worked?'"

He paused for effect, and Sarah sensed Rachel stiffen.

"Where was He, that One who claims to be your Father? Was He there watching and waiting and listening? Listening for the voice of His people: a cry of penitence, a cry for help? And had it . . ."

Beneath his voice came another sound—a deep humming, low, yet insistent—and he spoke louder, straining a little, and the girls saw in his face the signs of annoyance, but the sound did not go and grew clearer, coming closer, a powerful, regular throbbing, until there could be no doubt that it was the sound of a motorbike, and in order to be heard above it, the Father was shouting, the anger in his voice evident to all.

"Had they once called . . . Had they once, in their last moments, called out to me . . ."

His voice was drowned by the engine roar, now directly outside the church, and in the instant that he ceased shouting, abandoning what had become a contest, the noise was cut.

At first there was nothing, no further sound or movement, and the Father stood stiff. His congregation sat likewise. Then came footsteps, deliberate and even, and every head turned to follow his gaze toward the open door.

Sam appeared, his body framed against the dazzling morning.

For a space of seconds he hesitated, then, with a slight nod in the direction of the Father—who stood firm before his altar—he looked about, and seeing Rachel and Sarah in the back pew, he sat down beside them. He folded his arms and looked ahead, intending to listen.

There was nothing to hear. No sooner had the congregation turned its eyes to the front to wait, as it were, for the next move, than the Father opened his arms in an attitude of supplication to heaven and, with a mighty "Amen," vanished through a curtain behind the altar.

It was clear to all that the service had ended.

Women stood, stepped out into the aisle, bowed toward the altar, and filed past the girls. As each went by, she found reason to slow her pace, adjusting her sleeve or touching her hair—just long enough to look; to see at first hand this one who had walked in.

When the last had gone, leaving the church empty, Sam leaned forward, resting his elbow on the back of the pew in front, and gave the girls his crooked grin.

"Well, I thought coming into this place would be pretty painful, but it looks like I missed the worst of it."

"You didn't *miss* it," Sarah said, her eyes alive with delight. "You *were* it. You came here on purpose, didn't you—just to mess things up?"

Sam's expression changed. It was Rachel he was watching. She was not happy; not like Sarah.

"No," he said, turning to face the front and sitting back. "I didn't come to make trouble. I came because it was time that I did. Something happened after you left last night. About midnight someone came down, a young guy—big, with black hair slicked back. He was worked up about something and started slashing at my tent with a knife. He said he was . . ."

"The Angel," Sarah said. "It would have to be Angel Rossellini."

"Sure. That was the name. Angel. But he was no angel. Not to me, anyway. And he said to keep away from you." He nodded at Rachel. "That the Father— old Gray Eye—said that you were a pair. That you and this Angel were set up a long time ago, and that I had to get out. And while he was talking, he was slashing the tent. So we ended up in a fight. He could have done anything to me—he had the advantage with the knife, and he's one hell of a lot bigger than I am, but when he had me for sure, something happened, like he was disturbed—interrupted by someone—and he got up and left."

"Do you believe that about him and me?" Rachel said. "Do you believe all that?"

"How would I know? I don't understand this place. Or the people. I sure don't understand why they come at you with knives."

"They're mad," Sarah said. "I always said they were."

Rachel stood with her back to Sarah, cutting her off, and turned to look down at Sam.

"I'm sorry about what happened," she said. "About what Angel did with the knife, and your tent; but if you think that I would let myself get married off to him because the Father says so, then you don't understand me either."

She moved to push past, to get out into the aisle, but Sarah grabbed the back of her dress, holding her.

"Rachel," she said. "Stop it. You're acting like an idiot."

"I wasn't attacking you, Rachel," Sam said, turning to her. "And I never seriously thought that you would want to be with that guy. It was like he was crazy. All fired up about you—and me—and I'd never seen him before in my life. Why would he go for me like that? Even if you were his girl, why would he go for me like that? I only talked to you."

Rachel remained silent, but Sarah was ready to explain.

"It's nothing to do with Rachel. It's all in Angel's head. And the Father's. Angel decided years ago that Rachel was his. And the Father backs him up. The Angel doesn't go out on the boats, he only does shore work, on the jetties, and when he's finished, he comes up here and helps the Father do his garden. Nobody knows why he does that—maybe because they're as weird as each other—but that's how come Angel gets his head filled with what you heard; the Father talks to him—tells him things for his ears only—and the Angel believes it all. The Father arranges everything around here. He controls people's lives. All the superstition. Like those signs . . ."

Rachel leaned forward and gave her a look, and she said no more.

Sam stepped into the aisle. "So what's here for you?" he said. "Look at this place. I never saw anything like it. What are these walls? Crates? Shipping crates?"

"There's no local timber. No decent trees," Sarah volunteered. "The men get goods from all over. Pumps and winches and . . ."

"Look here. These names. They're from every-where." He turned, opening his arms to encompass the interior. "He's got every country here, your old Gray Eye . . . he's got the whole world here. Right in his own backyard. But this place can't last," he said, stopping. "It's pine. It's junk."

"It's varnished. The whole church gets done every year with marine varnish, just like the boats. Layer after layer."

"But you can't expect . . ." He did not finish. He had seen the window.

"Ah," he said. "So . . ." Then almost immediately, "Where's my face?"

Sarah got up and turned to Rachel. "See?" she said. "Now you've got him believing."

But Sam was not listening. He was walking toward the altar, looking up.

"Wait," Rachel said. "Don't go down. If the Father comes back . . ."

He ignored her. He reached the front row of pews, then the altar, and the girls were silent, watching, until Sarah said, "It's supposed to show Jesus. The fisher of men. He's supposed to be bringing in his net filled with the sinners that he saved."

She moved to the center of the church. "Only it isn't like that here. There's no gentle Jesus, meek and mild, in New Canaan. It's the Father who casts the net, and drags it in too. It's the dragging in that he likes the best. See all the miserable little bodies wriggling in it? They're the ones he's caught."

"Caught?" Sam said. "What do you mean 'caught'?"

"Trapped. Netted. Kept under his thumb."

She moved closer. "It doesn't matter what you call it, it all boils down to the same thing. Rachel and I, we come here because if we don't, he would come to our houses to see us there—alone—like he visits all the women. But he knows what we think of him. We only come because it saves trouble."

From where she sat, Rachel added, "Our mothers used to come every Sunday. And they made us. They cleaned his rooms too—in the back, behind the curtain—and this church. But they're . . ."

"Not here anymore." A voice from the entrance cut her off, and they turned to see the Father, in the doorway, exactly as Sam had appeared hardly five minutes before.

Instantly Rachel stood.

"Father," she said, her voice a model of control. "You were so quiet. This is Sam. He is from the city. We were showing him the church. The window."

The Father came forward, stepping out of the light into the gloom of the church. And as he came toward him, deftly sidestepping Sarah in the aisle, Sam saw the white of his robe and his face, the age of it, and thought, *Last night . . . the mask . . . the skull . . .* Then they met, face to face, before the altar.

"We have so few visitors here," the Father said. "I am sorry that this morning's service had to be curtailed. I was briefly overcome. An extraordinary thing. I shall have to visit all those who were here and have since left, ministering to them personally."

At this, his pale eyes swept the church, as if checking whether any of the faithful did, in fact, remain. He turned again to Sam.

"You were considering the window? Yes. It is a remarkable creation. A work of art. All local too. No outside labor at all. No. Nothing from outside in that. The binding lead is from the weights in our nets. The glass is from the homes of my people, except for certain pieces, dredged from the bottom of the lagoon, from the mud, broken bottles and the like. That is the dull or smoky glass. There and there."

He paused, pointing at the glass where the penetration of light was low, the colors lackluster.

"That is the glass which has been damaged by sedimentary pumice or sand. An abrasive action . . ."

The writhing figures snared in the net were of this glass, and there were others, Sam saw, dead black, not of glass at all, but an opaque substance—pottery or china—broken cups or saucers or plates. The limbs of these figures were angular and malformed.

Like crustaceans, Sam thought. *Horrible.*

But the Father had gone on, ". . . and thus their savior is of the sea, or from the sea, yet set high above it, against the heavens."

He paused, looking into Sam's face and smiling his thin smile. "But I have said too much. I believe that as I arrived, I was fortunate enough to hear our Sarah providing you with a very interesting interpretation of the window's meaning. I should allow her to continue. If she has more to say?"

Knowing well that he had hit home, he flicked his gaze at Sarah, her face burning in humiliation.

"Nothing?" he murmured, smiling still. "A pity . . ."

"But the fisherman," Sam said, "is he yourself? His robes are white like yours."

The Father laughed, sweeping his hands down to indicate his stature.

"Compare," he said. "He is a young man, tall and vigorous. And his hands—so strong, hauling his net. Yet, see?"

He held out his own hands, turning them, palms up and palms down, displaying the creamy texture of his skin, the bony leanness of his fingers, the nails, filed like crescent moons.

"These hands have never touched a net. No, I am not the figure in the glass. But now I must go. I must. If you would . . ." and he extended his arm to indicate the open door.

"Another thing," Sam said, taking no notice of the gesture and moving closer to the altar. "I heard that some see a third face there. Behind the kneeling women, there, in the folds of his robe. That's fascinating, don't you think?"

"What? They see what?"

"A face," Sam said. "Behind the two women—the two mourning Marys, I guess—another face. It's hard to . . ."

The girls had come forward, waiting.

"Nonsense," the Father said, though he looked up as he spoke.

Sam would not be put off. "But shouldn't there be another woman in that scene? Traditionally, aren't there three Marys? Mary the mother of Jesus and Mary the Magdalene and Mary the sister of Martha? That's what I was taught, where I come from."

The Father showed impatience, and his voice tightened. From where Sarah stood, slightly behind him and to the side, she saw a muscle twitch at the corner of his mouth.

"Of course there could have been another Mary there. And any number of others. Men or women. What does it matter? What is your point?"

"Nothing. No point. But I heard that someone had seen a face. Another face. And I heard that it looked like me. Funny. But I can't see . . ."

"Nonsense. That is nonsense. This window was made to my design. There was a gap between the women. An awkward space, filled with drapery. The glass was very poor. Very smoky. And there is also the light. In the afternoon with the sun behind, the colors are like jewels, the figures live and move . . . and then the mountain comes between, gets in the way—the core—and the shapes are distorted. You could see anything, imagine anything there—saints, angels, demons . . ."

Sarah came closer still, almost touching the altar with her sleeve. She had never seen the Father like this. Never seen him so unnerved.

"I wanted to know," Sam said, "because my mother came from here. Or I think that she might have. And if the face looked like mine, I thought . . ."

The Father moved to stand behind the altar, and there, set off against the white robe, Sam saw what appeared to be a crucifix.

Sarah leaned forward, whispering, "That thing . . . he calls it the icon."

It was an anchor of brass, perhaps fifteen inches high, mounted on a base of stone to give the appearance of a cross, and where the shaft intersected the cross member—which terminated in vicious barbs— there was a starburst of glinting rays. *Nails,* Sam thought, *brass nails out of a ship.* At its center, focused directly on Sam, was a single eye, enameled in black, its iris of gray.

"Now, here is a curious thing," the Father said, lowering his head to look one way, then the other, as if assessing the length of the altar.

"This icon is solid brass. Very heavy. Yet I am always realigning it, centering it, at least once daily. Often twice. I come in here, and I look, and it has moved of its own accord. The eye, you see. I face it toward the window, but it turns—outward, facing the door, the town. A very strange thing . . ."

He looked up, and turning the object to himself with great deliberation, he smiled again, allowing his lips to part, showing his teeth.

Yellow, Sam thought. *Like an animal's.*

"So," continued the Father, "you are a quester. One who searches. One with a mission. A wonderful thing, when you are young. I too . . ."

"I am looking for my mother," Sam said. "I was told that she might have come from here. I hoped you might help. Since this is the only church, I thought that you might know, or have records here. They say that her name was Hannah. They say she was black. Aboriginal. Part Aboriginal or Islander. I don't know anything for certain, not even her other name. If she came from New Canaan, or the country around here, it would have been nearly twenty years . . ."

"Black?" The Father raised his eyebrows. "Your mother?"

"Yes. So they say. I never knew her. That's the trouble."

"And your father?"

"I know nothing about him. But can you remember a girl called Hannah, or check? Are there records? A register?"

"For blacks? A record of blacks? Why would there be a record of them? They did not come here. Not to this church."

"But were they here? Around here?"

Then the Father's voice came low and even, its threat in its quietness.

"You know already where they were. I have seen you down by the lagoon, digging. I know. I have watched." He paused, his pale eyes burning into Sam's.

"But then, it depends on what you are looking for. What you really want to know. Everything depends . . ."

"Wait. Wait. I didn't come here to make trouble. I came here because this is a church, and you are . . . And there is supposed to be a book. I heard that there is a book."

From the corner of his eye, Sam saw the girls move. They stood together at the head of the aisle. The breath of the Father was hot in his face.

"A book? Yes. There is a book. There is a great book. And my girls here know it, and no doubt told you . . ."

"It was not the girls who told, it was . . ." But Sam did not finish. The Father raised his hand, and before Sam could prevent him or step aside, a thin finger was pressed momentarily against his lips.

"I will listen to no more. You have already come into my church, destroying my service with your noise. I have learned patience, but do not try me. Do not, as some say, press your luck."

He stepped back, setting a distance between them. He set his expression into a smile. "It is as I told your friend when he came with his questions."

"Jordy . . . John Jordan?"

"And a marvelous name too. A prophet's name, as you, with your knowledge of scripture, would recall. He asked at the depot and the jetties and the Fisherman's Rest. Would it be six months ago? Has it been that long? No matter. Now you come asking. I will tell you what he was told. I will tell you to your face. Your blacks have been gone for years. In the beginning they were here, camped by the lagoon, in their humpies and filth, near the mangroves. But one day they were gone. Just like that. Apart from the shells and rubbish that you have found yourself, they left nothing. Not a thing."

"But, Father, Sam is doing research for his degree. Can't you tell him anything about his family?"

Rachel had come to stand close beside Sam.

From the head of the aisle, Sarah added, "He has a right to know who he is."

"Ah." The Father placed his palms against his temples in a gesture of sudden revelation. "Ah. How foolish of me. Thank you, Sarah. What he must do is clear to me now. If he would find himself, let him look into his heart. Or a mirror. He has those choices. To look in, or out. What he decides depends on his own vanity. I can tell him that . . ."

"No," Sam began, "I'm not interested in saving myself, if that's what you mean."

The Father's hand was raised to silence him. "No more," he said. "No more. It is time that I rested. I am closing the church. You will go now."

He left the altar and, opening his arms, drove them out before him.

When the door had slammed shut and they stood in the porch, shaking their heads in confusion, Sarah whispered, "He's afraid. I'm sure of it."

IV

When Sarah left the church, heading home, Rachel walked down to the mangroves with Sam.

"What will you do about the tent?" she said when she saw it slashed and sagging.

He shrugged. "I don't know. Hibbert gave me the money for that too. I'm not going to ask her for any more."

He was kneeling beside his bike, packing its side bin, ready to leave. She stood next to him, watching. "Since I won't be coming down for much longer, maybe I could do without."

"You're not leaving because of what's happened?" she said. "Not because of the Father? Or Angel?"

He laughed and got up, reaching out to put his hands on her shoulders.

"No. Not because of them. Thugs like Angel were in and out of the home all the time. I'm used to types like him. As for the Father, well, I don't know. I wouldn't trust him. But about the tent, this morning when . . ."

She slipped her arms around his waist, catching her thumbs in the belt of his jeans.

He grinned. "Hmmm . . . Well . . . As I was saying, this morning when I was walking up to the church, I had a look at some of those empty boatsheds. I wondered if I could stay in one of them until I'm finished. I could keep the bike there too. Out of sight. It wouldn't be for long. Maybe two or three more . . ."

She stepped away, shaking her head. "No," she said. "Not there. You can't stay anywhere near where Angel goes. He isn't joking when he says he'll get you. I've seen him in fights before. He'll come looking, and those sheds are too close. No. You can't stay there."

He knelt in the sand and went on with his packing. "What am I supposed to do, then? I need some cover. I can't leave everything out in the open. It's not just my bike. It's all this equipment, my notes and drawings. And besides, I want to finish, write everything down properly." He was looking up now. "Whatever happens about finding where I come from, well, that's one thing. But getting the research on this dig written, that's another. I really want to do that. I want to write what they call an occasional paper. It's like a pamphlet, a little book. The university bookshop publishes them. I don't want to chuck everything in because of him."

"There's the quarry at the core," she said, half to herself. "There's a couple of places up there where nobody goes."

Then, warming to the idea, she knelt beside him to help. "There's sheds where you could stay and some deep caves where you could leave the bike. You could go up there. That would be all right. It's not far, around behind the lantana, and up past the cemetery. Ten minutes walk from here. I could call you. If you gave me a number where I could reach you, I could use the phone at the store and let you know if there's a place before you come down."

When Sam had gone, wheeling his bike up through the tea trees, she went home and busied herself with routine Sunday jobs, trying to put him and all that had happened out of her head. She made her father's lunch and prepared his dinner, packing it for him to take out that night, and after he left for the men's service on the jetty, she cleaned up in the kitchen and changed the linen on his bed.

Sarah came around about six, and they sat together on the verandah, talking.

But when Rachel was alone again and had showered and dressed ready for bed, she was not at ease;

there was a clamminess in her hands and something like the flush of fever in her face, and she knew that even if she went to bed, even if she dropped on top of the sheets that she had laundered herself and turned down already, she would never be able to sleep.

She went to the verandah and stood with her forehead against the screens, peering out. Beyond the gate the sandy track led down to the lagoon where the moon would be silver across the water. She smiled, thinking where that silver would break into eddies in the shallows among the mangroves. This was a new and secret smile, as if to say "Why not?" and since there was no one about likely to answer, she went back into the house and down the dim hallway to her parents' room. She turned to the darkest corner and opened the mirrored door of a wardrobe. She reached into the blackness of the hanging space and, knowing exactly where her hand would find it, removed a dress of plain gray jersey. Her mother had made this for a wedding but never worn it, since it was smooth and sensual, and the Father, who had asked to see it when he called, would not allow her, saying that it was underclothing, and not a thing for a woman to be seen in. Still, Eva Burgess had kept the dress, hiding it in the darkness at the back of her wardrobe, where her daughter found it, silky and mysterious as ever.

Rachel stepped out of her pajamas and slipped the

dress over her head to feel the magic as it slithered down her body, tingling and cool against her skin.

Then she was gone, out of the house and along the sandy track, the night wind from the lagoon cooling her face and catching her hair, and her smile broke into a laugh in the delight of independence. She knew New Canaan well enough; no one would be about on a Sunday night. It was not a night for visiting; she could go wherever she liked, unnoticed. Especially in this dress, which was the color of moonlight.

But as she reached the tea trees and paused, wondering whether she should turn left to the mangroves or right, away from the lagoon to the open beach, she was certain that she heard the Father's voice and looked about in amazement, knowing that she had not heard, not in reality, although she waited, listening for more. *Nothing,* she said to herself. *Absolutely nothing.* She took the tea-tree path.

Down past the depot and the first of the boatsheds she went, stopping sometimes to look out across the water, and when the side track to the jetties appeared, she took it without hesitation. Only then did she realize where she was going—or being led. Here was the jetty where her mother had died, and again she heard the voice, echoing the words of the Father's sermon that day: "And where was He when Eva Burgess was struck, pierced by the serpent . . ."

Now there was no spring in her step, no swing of

assurance in her arms, only foreboding, and she heard "Where was He, that One who claims to be your Father?" and wondered for the thousandth time, *Why?* What had her mother done that nothing less than death could atone for her wickedness?

At the end of the jetty, she leaned on the handrail and looked out at the bar. She was stupid, she thought, for coming here and exposing herself to hurt, and she grew vaguely uneasy, taken by the sensation that she was no longer alone, that there was something moving in the darkness behind her. She turned, but there was nothing. Then she caught the flicker of a movement from the direction of the mangroves, not a light exactly—although it could have been—but more the fluttering of a wing; probably the herons. She took little notice, but when it came again, and then again, she turned bodily and saw that far over across the lagoon there was something on the mangrove bank, near Sam's camp. Though she moved to that side of the jetty and peered into the darkness, she could make out nothing distinctly, no more than a shining or waving movement which was not coming from any bird, and certainly not from Sam. Moonlight dress or not, out there she was too visible, and she made for the cover of the trees.

If anyone was there, it would be the Angel. He was the type who would return to see what more damage he could do—or gloat over what he had already done.

She did not take the tea-tree path for fear of meeting him but moved through the scrub slightly inland, where there were pockets of darkness and stands of silvery trunks that she could slip among to disappear.

When she entered the clump of banksias that marked the end of her protection, she stopped and said to herself, *Rachel, what do you think you're hiding from?* And setting her shoulders, she stepped out into the moonlit clearing.

Almost at once she saw what was causing the trouble—the remains of Sam's tent, abandoned on the sand, waving and flapping in the night wind.

Just great, she thought, shaking her head, and with a shrug of disgust she was about to go when out of the darkness above the banksias the herons rose suddenly, as they had the first time she had disturbed Sam. She dropped down off the bank and, lifting her head above the edge, saw the Father emerge from the tea-tree path and pass around the shadowy rim of the clearing in the direction of the lantana.

So, she thought, *I am not so crazy.* Keeping low, she followed the muddy strip past the remains of the tent, where she hitched up her mother's dress to climb the bank, and once on top, she crept into the cover of the bush. But when she looked back, the Father had vanished. There was only the moonlit sand of the clearing, the stark mangroves, and the darkness of the lantana beyond.

She moved inland, hoping that she might glimpse
him again, but the farther she went from the lagoon,
the denser the bush became. This was not the open
bush of the shore, filtered by the wind off the water;
here the air was rank with humus, and the stems of
the lantana scratched her and caught her hair and
dress, and more than once she was forced to stop
and free herself. Still she went on, pushing through
until the entanglements became so thick that she
knew the Father could not have come this way at all.
She turned back, following the trail of crushed lantana, almost sick from the heavy night smell of it. She
was glad to walk out, at last, into the sweet wind off
the lagoon.

Sarah's, she thought. *That's where I'll go. It can't be
that late. She'll be up. I'll go there and tell her to make me
coffee or cocoa. Maybe she can make sense of all this.*

Dropping down onto the mud, to keep out of sight
below the bank, she followed the narrow beach
around the lagoon to the boatsheds, then slipped once
more into the cover of the tea trees.

V

But no light shone from Sarah's house, not even from
her room, and Rachel stood in the yard, wondering
what to do. She could go to her window and knock on

it, to wake her, or she could leave; it was late, and they would be together in the morning. She knew that she should go home . . . get out of her mother's dress—which was ruined, she was certain—take a shower to get rid of the black mangrove mud smeared all over her, and do something about the scratches on her arms, which had started to sting; so she turned toward the path, intending to go, but a movement on the verandah caught her eye. There was someone up there, behind the screens, watching.

"Sarah?" she whispered. "Is that you?"

There was no answer.

"Sarah . . .?"

As she stepped closer, into a patch of moonlight, she heard, "Eva . . ."

The word drifted down. "Eva . . ."

Someone had called her mother's name. She moved closer, her hand against her mouth. It came again. "Eva . . ."

Then she saw. Behind the screens stood Miriam Goodwin.

"Eva . . ." she said. "Eva, come in."

"Sarah!" Rachel yelled. "Sarah, quick!"

Miriam fumbled at the screen door catch.

"Sarah. Quick. It's your mother."

There was the click of a switch, the verandah flooded with light, and Sarah emerged from the hallway.

"What?" she said, pushing handfuls of hair out of

her eyes. "What? Oh . . . geez . . . Mum."

The screen door opened, and Miriam stepped down toward Rachel, standing frozen at the foot of the stairs.

"Eva, you came. I knew. I was waiting."

She reached to touch Rachel's face.

"No, Mum." Sarah grabbed her from behind, pulling her back. "It's Rachel. It's only Rachel." And with a nod for Rachel to come in, she led her mother down the hall, speaking softly all the while, until a door closed somewhere in the darkness.

When Sarah appeared again, she held a hand against her lips, signaling quiet, and with the other motioned for Rachel to follow. She led the way into her room, turning on the light but leaving the door ajar behind her.

"Mum spoke . . ." she began, then, for the first time, she saw Rachel clearly. She stared in amazement at the dress, the mud, and the scratches.

"What on earth . . .?"

Rachel shook her head. "I'll tell you everything when you get me a drink. Cocoa. Let me get my breath for a minute. You make me a cocoa and I promise that I'll tell you everything. OK?"

Sarah left without argument, and Rachel sat on the arm of the great chair that faced the window. She saw herself reflected there, looking the mess that she did, and behind her and about her, likewise reflected, was the room with its warmth of red wood. She leaned forward to touch the cold glass.

"So," Sarah said, coming in and seeing her. "Admiring ourselves, are we?"

She pushed a mug of cocoa into her friend's hand. "You look like Cinderella after the stroke of twelve. Stay there. I'll sit on the rug and listen."

"No," Rachel said. "You take the chair. There's a lot to work out. I might need to walk. And no questions until I've finished."

So Sarah sat in her chair while Rachel walked and talked, stopping now and then to sip the cocoa, until all of the night's doings were told, from her restlessness to her experience in the lantana.

"But why the lantana?" Sarah said when she knew that Rachel was done. "What would the Father be doing near the lantana? Unless it's because of that sign. The hourglass . . ." But she stopped suddenly, looking up. "Mum . . ."

The reflection in the window showed her mother standing in the doorway behind them.

"The hourglass," Miriam said, entering the room, "above the lantana," and she crossed directly to Rachel, her bare feet soundless on the polished wood.

Her fingers touched Rachel's hair, and from it fell the tiny trumpet flowers of the lantana, which she caught in the palm of her hand, their yellows and carmines shining brighter by the light.

"You see, Eva," she said, "like jewels," then, lifting her head to stare at her reflection, "or the colored glass in his window."

She tipped her hand and the flowers fell to be lost in the bright fabric of the rug.

"Mum," Sarah said, standing, but her mother ignored her and turned again to Rachel.

"And was he there? Was the Father down there?"

"I'll go," Rachel said. "I shouldn't have come."

She went to leave, but the woman was not done. She stepped forward, blocking Rachel's way.

"Eva, tell me that you're back. That you came back to watch with me. To wait. It won't be long."

"Mrs. Goodwin," Rachel began, "Mrs. Goodwin, don't . . ." A hand was firm on her forearm, squeezing.

"Leave her alone, Mum," Sarah said with conviction. "Let her go."

The hand fell away.

"This time you will go to bed and stay there. Rachel, you'd better go. I'll see you in the morning."

For the second time that night, Sarah led her mother away.

Wise Women

I

The following morning Rachel had hardly begun the sort when she heard her name called and looked up to see Sarah running along the jetty. She dropped what she was doing and ran back to meet her.

"What's wrong?" she said. "What? Tell me!"

Realizing that Sarah was too out of breath to say anything, she sat her down on an upturned crate and knelt in front of her.

"Now, stop for a minute and breathe steadily. Your trouble is that you need more exercise. You sit in that chair too much. And get your hair out of your mouth or you'll end up choking. There. Is that better?"

"A bit. I ran all the way from the house. It's Mum. She's gone. I have to . . ."

"What to do you mean, gone?"

"She had a terrible night. I could hear her in her room, talking."

"Again?"

"Yes, but only nonsense. Every time I went in, she was sitting up, going on and on, then this morning her bed was empty. I checked all through the house. Nothing. She must be in her nightie still. And her slippers are gone. The red felt ones. They were next to the bed."

"But . . ."

"I can't talk. I have to go. I have to get Dad and Joseph. Have you seen them?"

"They're down at your shed."

"And your dad?"

"Still on the boat."

"OK. I'm all right now. I'll get Dad to look up around the store, and Joseph can do along the ocean beach. If you can get your dad to start the sort, we could do the lagoon. The paths. Down to the lantana."

"Why the lantana?"

"Because you should have heard what she said last night. She said there would be a sign. And I said, 'What sign?' And she said, 'A sign in the earth . . . from the core to the lantana.' See? And I bet she's down there now, in the bush, where that hourglass was. I have to go. Will you . . . ?"

Rachel nodded. "I'll tell Dad. Meet you back here in a couple of minutes."

With a quick hug for reassurance, they separated.

II

They found the red slippers on a mangrove stump down from Sam's camp, near the lantana.

"She wants me to find her," Sarah said. "Why else would she leave them sitting here like that?"

Rachel shook her head. "The soles are clean. She's only worn them on the sandy track, so far. But from here on . . . there's only the lantana."

Beneath the thick, dull leaves, brambly stems twisted and rubbed. Sarah shuddered.

"Near here . . . Here . . . Here's where I went in last night. See the leaves wilting. And here."

Rachel dropped to the ground at the edge of the thicket.

"See . . . those little flowers. Everywhere. I didn't do that. She's come here and pulled the flowers off, in handfuls. See?"

Sarah was gone. She had drawn in her breath and pushed into the thicket.

Inside, each stem rasped and stripped the skin.

"Sarah," Rachel pleaded, "this is stupid. I've tried to get through. You can't . . ."

From ahead came the answer, "If Mum did, then I can."

And shortly after, "Go back if you want. You go back."

There was no more, only grunts and curses, until she caught her hair and Rachel stumbled into her, pulling at the tangle with both hands. "Sarah," she said, "come back. There has to be another way. She didn't come this way. She couldn't have."

"Well, someone's been here before me," she said, wrenching free. She was about to go on when she gasped as if she were stung.

"What?" Rachel said. "What's happened?"

Sarah lifted one arm to protect her face, then lunged forward, her free arm extended.

"See."

Hanging from her hand was a white cotton night-dress, covered with dirt and spotted with blood.

"That's hers," she said. "That's hers. Rachel. She's dead. She's . . ."

"Rubbish. Look at the blood on me." Rachel held out her arms. "And look at yourself. She would be the same. We're all scratched and bleeding. Give it to me."

She took the nightdress, shaking it out as best she could.

"See? They're only spots. She's taken it off. That's what she's done. She's got caught up and taken it off." She pushed past Sarah as she spoke, bending low.

"Here," she said. "Look down here."

At ground level was a tunnel, like the entry to a warren or a lair.

"She's taken that off so she can crawl through. She

has got down and crawled. She must be through here somewhere."

She went in herself, dropping on her hands and knees, and this time it was Sarah who called, "Wait, wait," since she was bigger and could not keep up. But they went on, the dead and fallen stems jabbing their palms and ripping at their knees, the heavy smell of crushed leaves filling their lungs, fogging their heads.

Then they were through. The gloom of the tunnel ended and suddenly there was sunlight. Rachel was first, falling forward on her elbows, and Sarah behind, following blindly, so that she fell too, and they looked up together, blinking away the glare.

In the center of a clearing—hardly a body length away—knelt Miriam Goodwin, naked, the shocking white of her skin smeared with blood. She was digging, sifting the surrounding sand and debris with her bare hands, shoving her fingers between the black rocks that lay partially exposed at her knees. She paused, looking up, but showed no sign of surprise.

"They're all under here," she said, quite calmly. "Under the sand. Under the rock. Right where they put them."

Then she resumed her digging. Even after Sarah scrambled forward and held her, rocking and stroking her, saying "Mum, Mum" over and over, she would not stop, her hands constantly probing in the sand, until Rachel said, "Sarah. That's enough. Here. Put this back on her," and while Sarah took the nightdress and attempted to dress her mother, Rachel looked away.

They were in a circular clearing, surrounded on all sides by lantana. Rachel felt the rock beneath her knees and glanced down. There was a thin layer of sand, littered with twigs and leaves, then a layer of rock, not basalt from the core, nor the pumice that washed up in the lagoon, but the black rock of the headland. *This rock was brought here*, Rachel thought, *and the lantana can't grow where the rock has been laid.*

Then Sarah called, "Rachel, here," and she crawled over to help. She lifted the woman's arms and looked at her hands. She saw the nails split to the quick and guessed that she had tried to prise the stones up. *Why?* she thought. *What could be under there?*

When her mother was dressed, Sarah said, "What do we do now? We can't take her out through that tunnel thing."

Rachel pointed upward, over the lantana. "If we're that close to the core," she said, indicating the peak that towered over them, "then the cemetery must be on the other side of this. Give me a minute."

Before Sarah could protest, she had vanished, calling as she went, "Wait. Just wait."

There was silence and, in no time, a shout.

"It's like a labyrinth in here. There are paths everywhere."

Then nothing. "Wait, I can see palings, an old fence. There are headstones. It comes out in the cemetery. I'm coming back. We'll make it, don't worry."

When they were out and had gone through the cemetery toward the cypresses and the town itself, Sarah said, "Rachel, you go on ahead. If there's anyone, even if it's Dad or Joseph, come back and let me know. I don't want anyone to see her. Not like this. It wouldn't be right."

Rachel understood.

III

That night, and during the week that followed, though Rachel stopped by, Sarah asked to be left alone with her mother.

"Rachel," she said, "I don't want you to have to do all of the sort by yourself, but what can I do? I'm not game to leave her, not the way she is. And Dad and Joseph aren't going to stay in and mind her."

"She needs proper help," Rachel said. "She needs a doctor."

"But if I call a doctor, he'll take her. And then what will happen to her? It wouldn't make her any better, sticking her in some hospital, would it?"

"It might."

"But where would that leave me? Here with the men."

"And me."

"That goes without saying. You know that. Just give me a week. You do the sort until the end of this week and leave me to look after her. There must be things in her, all mixed up in her head. Awful things. If I can stay with her and get her to talk—to me, I mean, not just herself—she could get better."

Rachel accepted rather than agreed. And Sarah tried everything.

First she stroked and patted. Beside her mother's chair on the verandah, she took her hand, saying nothing; simply being there. Other times she read to her: Psalms or Beatitudes or extracts from the Song of Solomon, or, once, a piece from the Book of Ruth: "Entreat me not to leave you, or to return from following after you: for where you go, I will go and there will I be buried. . . ." But nothing came of it.

Then there was talk. "Mum, I am sorry. Sorry that I accused you and said that you let me down. Sorry that I was too stupid to see how bad things were for you. I know now why you told me about that money you had hidden. I found it and took it, but I can't use it. I can't go away. I understand better now. I can see what Dad is, and Joseph. I see that they're useless. They're like bags on your back, big wet sandbags, that's what they're like, weighing you down, every day. I saw Dad's face when I brought you home. He looked at the scratches and . . . nothing. That's what. Nothing."

She tried to shock. She had Rachel bring lantana, stems of it, covered in flower heads. She pulled the flowers off and dropped them in her mother's lap, crushing the leaves to release the heavy smell.

"The lantana," she said. "Eva is in the lantana. The Father is in the lantana."

But apart from the shifting of her chair, to turn her back squarely against the sea, Miriam Goodwin gave no response, nor any hint that she would cease her tireless waiting.

Night after night Sarah would go into her room, drop into her chair, dig her toes into her rug, and look out at the sea through the gap in the dunes, her head pounding, saying to herself, over and over, *What do I do now? What?*

On the Friday afternoon while she was sitting on the back step reading and her mother dozed in her chair, Sarah looked up and there was Rachel coming through the gate, followed by Sam, wheeling his bike.

"How come you're here already?" she said, getting up. "It's only Friday."

"Rachel called me and I told her I would be down early. There's quite a few things to do at the dig. I heard about your mother. I'm sorry."

"I told him," Rachel said. "That's all right, isn't it?"

"Why not? It's not going to hurt her. Come in. I'll get something to drink."

"Give me a minute," Sam said, pushing his bike

closer to the house. "I want to leave this where I can see it. I don't trust your friend, the Angel. He's the type who could turn up anywhere."

Rachel came in. "When he's done that," she said, squeezing past Sarah on the stairs, "can you show him your room? I already told him about it. I can get the drinks." She went through into the kitchen.

Sarah waited, holding the screen door open, and when the bike was parked to his satisfaction, out of sight of the gate, Sam looked up at her watching him, winked, and grinned.

"What? You'd like a bike like that, would. . ." His face suddenly changed and he lifted his hand, pointing.

"Sarah . . ."

There was her mother, standing at her shoulder, staring down at him.

"Not again. Mum, do you have to?"

She turned back to Sam. "Sorry. I'll have to take her in. You come on through. Rachel's in the kitchen." Reaching for her mother's elbow, she attempted to lead her into the hallway.

"Come on. You better lie down."

But there was resistance. Miriam Goodwin was looking directly at Sam, her forehead creased, striving for recognition.

"No," she said. "Wait. Who is this one, now? Is it Hannah? Is she here too? Then it is time. It is surely the time."

Then, without hesitation, she stepped down and took Sam in her arms, patting his back with the flat of her hand.

Over her shoulder he saw Sarah standing amazed and Rachel in the hallway, an empty tray dangling from her hand.

"Mrs. Goodwin," he said, trying to move away, "I'm Sam. Hannah was my mother."

She appeared not to hear and, releasing him, turned deliberately to Sarah, whispering, "If Eva's back, and Hannah, then surely it's the time."

And she went to her room.

Sam stood where he was, half in, half out of the house. The screen door hung open. He looked from one to the other.

"You heard that. You both heard that. She said it, didn't she? Hannah? My mother's name? Didn't she?"

They had seen and heard.

"Get her back. Can't she tell me any more?"

"She might . . ." Sarah began, making no attempt to move.

"She couldn't just come out and say that. I mean, she couldn't make it up. She couldn't, could she?"

Sarah shook her head. "It's what she thinks she sees. Something must remind her. Something about how you look."

"Which proves that the Father is a liar," Rachel said.

"What about the rest of them?" Sam asked. "What about the ones Jordy talked to when he came down?

The ones at the pub, and the store?"

"The same," Sarah said. "All liars. Or all gutless."

"Or all stupid," Rachel added.

"No," Sam said, closing the screen door gently. "Not stupid. Something else. Afraid maybe. It could be they're afraid. Not talking." He looked directly at Sarah.

"Like my mum," she said.

Rachel nodded. "Maybe. But if your mum knew Hannah, then mine did too. She must have. All the locals must have, including the Father. You couldn't come from here and not be known. And if she's right about that, she could be right about other things. Like what my mother had to do with the lantana. And why your mother talked about the Father and that place. And why she's in there digging up rocks, cutting herself to bits to get to . . ."

"My mother wouldn't be the only black. Even if they all left, like the Father said. She wouldn't be the only one left."

"Or get pregnant by herself," Rachel concluded.

There was silence.

Sarah dropped into her mother's chair and leaned forward, resting her head in her hands, rubbing her eyes with her fingertips. Sam sat on the floor beside her, looking out. Rachel paced, dragging one finger along the screens.

Sarah looked up. "As far as I can tell," she said, "this

is all to do with the Father. I've been home all week, thinking. He came every day to see my mum. He sat out here, his chair up close, holding her hand and whispering in her ear, so soft that I couldn't hear a thing, and if I tried to listen or came around, he stopped. That's not open. That's not the way. All whispers and secrets. That's not religion. I've been sitting here thinking that Old Gray Eye might not be such a joke after all. That he might be dangerous. And his church. And his great book."

"The locals must believe anything. Look at that Angel. He believes what he's told. I just passed him now, up there working in that garden in the church. He's just a stooge, like all the rest. And as for that so-called great book, why can't it be a lie too?"

"But there is a book. It must exist. It can't be just hot air. Our mothers saw it, didn't they, Rachel? When they went up to clean. They talked about it. Very quiet. They would sit out here and talk. They knew things. And it's time I knew too. I've been thinking that I should wise up. I should find out . . ."

"How? Go up to him in the church like Sam last week and say, 'Oh, Father. I was wondering. Can I see your book? I need a few answers.' That won't get you far. But there's something else. What's under those rocks in the lantana? As soon as I saw your mother digging at them, the way she tried to get under, I thought, *There's something going on here.* That's why I called Sam and asked him down early, because I think he might know. Or be able to find out." She stopped pacing. They were watching her, waiting.

"The rocks in the lantana are from the headland. I know, I've seen them up there a hundred times. They're round and black, and they shine when they're wet. They're not basalt and they're not pumice. They're not from this side of the lagoon. So someone has put them in there. In a circle. Either they have put them there and then the lantana grew around them—but couldn't grow on them—or someone cleared that patch in the lantana and laid them there. I don't know. But why put them there? What are they covering up?"

"What do you mean, 'covering up'? How do you know . . .?"

"While you were dressing your mother, I saw. All she wanted was to get under those rocks. To lift them. Didn't you see her fingernails, broken to bits? And what she said. 'They're all under here. Under the rock.' You were busy. You mightn't have heard. But I did. And I saw too. And I want Sam to see. I want to get him down there. He does that sort of thing. He's used to digging."

He had watched her without expression, never taking his eyes from her face. Now he got up and crossed the verandah to stand in front of her, taking her hands in his.

"Hey," he said. "Hey. I hope you haven't got me

confused with someone else here. I hope you don't think that I'm some detective. Some forensic scientist. I'm in my first year of anthropology. This fieldwork is only one subject. Besides, I didn't understand half of what you were talking about. I'm not up on all this local stuff. OK?"

She could not look at him. She turned her head away to the screens. She was fighting back tears.

Sarah watched, thinking, *This is my Rachel? In tears? With a boy?*

He said, "It's getting late. I don't even have a place to stay. How about you forget about all this and show me the quarry or wherever hole-in-the-wall place I'm supposed to put my gear?"

He turned to Sarah. "I think we had better go. I'll see you tomorrow."

He went to the screen door and opened it, holding it for Rachel. Sarah sat and watched them leave.

IV

Once they were outside the gate and she was certain Sarah could not see, Rachel turned to Sam.

"You spoke to me in there as if I were a child," she said. "As well as that, you did it in front of my friend."

He had been walking his bike, and now he stopped, looking at her in astonishment.

"Sorry," he said. "It's just that . . ."

"I know. You think that this place is crazy. I think so too. So does Sarah. Give us credit for some brains. The point is that, until lately, it didn't really matter to us what anyone in New Canaan believed about the Father and the book and everything else that goes on here. We thought that we would get out and go to college or find a job in the city. But now we're stuck here, we both want to know what's going on. That's what I started to tell you on the phone, and again back there. Sarah has got her own ideas, but if you would let me show you this place in the lantana, the clearing where we found her mother, I might know more about what's happening."

"OK. Sure. I believe you." He kicked the stand down on his bike and faced her.

"Now it's my turn. And you listen, all right? Last Sunday I swam across the lagoon and I sat on the rocks on the other side and looked back. There was the spire of the church, sticking up, and there was that mountain right beside it. The core. Huge. Rising right out of the earth. See? And when I went down to pay the Father a visit, and I saw his miserable packing case church and its tacky varnish, I knew straight off that all that kept it standing were the rocks stacked up the side. Then there was that fisherman's window. Have you ever seen proper stained glass?"

She shook her head.

"I thought so. Rachel, you have to believe me, that Father, he's a fake. A con man. Apart from finding out about my mother, this whole business with him has got nothing to do with me. I'm sick of it. I came down here to do an assignment demonstrating the scientific method, and I end up back in the Dark Ages. What a joke."

He turned to his bike.

"Sam," she said.

He sighed, waiting.

"In this place where I want you to look, in the lantana, there is a round clearing covered in sand. Just under the sand are rocks from the headland. Only small, but the same black rocks. They seem to be placed very carefully. You could hardly get your fingers between them. This might not have anything to do with my mum, or Sarah's. And probably nothing to do with the Father. Leave him right out of it. All that makes no difference. But the rocks are there. Someone has put them there very carefully. Now, I'm saying that you should get in there and take a look, because maybe your people did this. You see? Maybe your oyster eaters did this."

"What?"

"I'm saying that these rocks might be part of the midden site."

"Rachel . . ."

"They might be like a ring of rocks for cooking . . . like a great oven."

"But . . ."

"Well?"

"Sure. It could be."

"Can I show you?"

"Sure. But . . ."

"It's too late now. Tomorrow's Saturday. I'll be working in the morning. I could take you after that."

He nodded. "OK. If I can get some more done on my notes before you come down."

"Right," she said, trying to appear composed yet barely concealing her self-satisfied smile.

Suspecting that he had been tricked, he narrowed his eyes—but she went on quickly, and the moment passed.

"Now, before it gets dark, we should sort out where you're spending the night. When you came in and passed the Angel, did he see you?"

"He saw me. He was right beside the garden wall, staking some plants. He watched me until I turned onto the track to your place."

"Did he say anything?"

"He didn't have to. He had that knife on his belt and he kept his hand on it. I got the message."

"He always wears it. It's supposed to be a fishing knife." She came closer, leaning against the saddle of his bike. "Well, you will have to go out that way." She indicated the direction of the church. "The same way that you came in. Ride past him as if you're leaving. I'll meet you on the other side of the cypresses. Past the boundary."

"What? Now?"

"Unless you want him coming after you. Make it seem like you're leaving. Like you came for a quick visit."

"So where am I supposed to ride to?"

"I can go down the tea-tree path and cut across and come up onto the road through the bush. Look out for me on the side of the road. Then I can take you up to the sheds at the quarry."

"What if you're not there? Or I get out there before you?"

She took a few steps backward down the lane. "I'll make sure that you see me. It takes five minutes to cut across there. I know this place. I was born here."

"Big deal . . ." He grinned and pushed the bike off. "I almost was . . ."

V

She heard the roar of his bike and stepped out from the bushes, flagging him down. He was wearing his helmet, and while he raised and lowered his eyebrows and rolled his eyes, playing the fool, she yelled, "Don't turn it off. Go up the road farther. Let it sound like you're leaving, and we can walk back. Wait till I get on."

He nodded vigorously to show approval, and when her arms were tight around him, he gunned the engine and took off, feeling her hands pull back

against his ribs. But not for long. Where the long afternoon shadow of the core fell across the road, she
tapped on his helmet, and he decelerated, then cut
the engine entirely, cruising to a stop on the narrow
shoulder. He lifted the visor of his helmet and half-
turned to her.

"OK, Miss Mastermind, what now?"

She slipped from the saddle. "We walk back a bit.
There's a track through the swamp to the base of the
core. That's where the quarry is, and there's sheds
where you could stay. All right?"

The track was barely discernible. Clumps of swamp
grasses had grown across it and tea-tree saplings shot
up from its peaty bed. Rachel walked ahead, navigat-
ing; Sam wheeled the bike, cursing.

"We're nearly there," she assured him. "We're
nearly there . . . almost," until he saw a rusted gate,
hanging askew, and wired to it a sign, likewise rusted,
declaring this place to be the Core Quarry.

"See," she said, lifting the gate open. "You're not
likely to get found here."

He glanced back down the track. "No, and I probably won't find my way out again either. Where the
hell am I?"

She called him through and made an attempt at
closing the gate, "To make it look undisturbed," she
said, and then she nodded toward the core, its rock
face hardly a hundred yards from them.

"For a start, use the core as your marker, and over

there, behind those sheds and bushes, there's the quarry, then more of this swampy bush, then the cemetery, the lantana, and your old camp. It's not far. I came here to check."

He had moved on, looking up at the great rock looming above.

"The sheds are through there," she said, following him. "Behind that scrub."

"Where's the quarry?"

"Right at the base of the rock. And there's a pool— or spring, I suppose you would call it. It's never had a proper name."

"A proper name? What sort of a name is a proper name?"

"Everything around here is named. The lagoon. The core. The cypresses. The tea-tree path. It's just one of those things. In the beginning the Father named everything."

He stopped and turned, resting on his bike. "In the beginning? In what age? The Palaeozoic . . . the Meso-zoic?"

"It was only an expression. It's what they say here."

"You mean, what they believe here—that's more like it. They believe that arrogant old fart is some sort of god."

"You can't say what they believe," she said, step-ping up to him. "You don't know what my father believes. What my mother . . ."

"I'm not putting your parents down. I've never

even met them. But half an hour ago you were saying these people were all liars and stupid. Now you're defending them. And all this about names. Your friend the Angel said the same thing. Your names are in the book. What, did the Father name you too?"

Immediately she looked away.

"Rachel. He didn't!"

She turned back and shrugged. "He named every one of us. My father and mother and Sarah and her father and mother. And her brother. Everyone. He named us all."

"And if he names you and puts you in his book, he owns you. Is that it?"

"I wouldn't say too much if I were you. You said that Hibbert named you. You said that you had no name at all, that she gave you both your names. And just for the record, nobody owns me, and they never will."

She walked on toward the core, but as she passed him—staring at her—she patted him on the shoulder.

"Come on. The quarry sheds are over this way."

He followed her as she picked the best path through weedy outcrops of groundsel and castor-oil bush until the evidence of abandoned industry grew increasingly obvious: cable rolls and drums and winches and derricks lay everywhere, and scattered throughout were flat-roofed sheds of timber and corrugated iron streaked with rust, each with a door still hasped and padlocked.

"All their windows are broken," he said. "The doors are bolted, but the windows are gone."

He left his bike and walked among them, peering in. "Do you reckon I could stay in one of these?"

"There's a bigger one," she said. "At the base of the rock."

The building was long and low, enclosed with shattered louvers. Inside, it was littered with the remains of desks and chairs and shelving. The walls were scrawled with obscenities.

"This must have been the office," he said. "But who got to this place? Who made this mess?"

"I wouldn't know. Nobody comes here. They quarried basalt for outside sale, but some was used for buildings in town. You saw the church. The buttresses. And the foundations. All the houses in town are built on stone from the core. So is the store, and there's a whole wall behind the bar in the Fisherman's Rest. But all that building was finished years ago. I don't know who would have been here since. Maybe the Steele boys. They used to get around."

"The Steele boys?"

"They drowned at the beginning of this year. Caught up in their father's net. . . . They were the only other kids left here. Or the Angel might have done this years ago. I don't know."

He turned away, looking back toward the gate.

"Is there anywhere else? Somewhere not so attractive to loonies?"

"Around the back. Near the quarry."

Again she led the way, following the suggestion of a path that looped behind the building, and there, with no preliminary inclination of the earth or surround of scattered boulders, was the base of the core.

"Look," he said, walking toward it. "We were that close."

He touched the rock with his fingers, then ran his palm over it.

"Strange." He put his hand to his chin. "It's like skin. Stubbly skin."

He turned to her, standing behind, watching.

"It's nothing like I thought. Not like rock at all. From the lagoon it looked smooth and hard, like metal. But it's not at all."

He touched it again. "It's like skin. Almost soft. Like there's something beneath. Flesh maybe."

"It wasn't always like this," she said. "It was covered in thorns. All over. Ever since I can remember. Then this year there was a fire . . ." She did not bother to finish. He was not listening.

With one hand constantly touching or trailing against its face, he negotiated the broad curve of the base of the rock. From time to time he would turn, not so much to check that she was there but to give her the widest grin, as if to say, "This is terrific. I'm glad I'm doing this." She was happy to follow, knowing what was coming: his first sight of the quarry and the pool beneath.

About fifty yards from the abandoned office, the path veered away from the rock and vanished among thick grasses. Great blocks of weathered basalt lay scattered here, tumbled among the grass or protruding from it, all angles and facets. Some were stacked, one on top of the other in pyramids; others, draped in creepers, ran in lengths like ancient walls. He stopped between these, their parallel surfaces dwarfing him.

Without turning he said, "Did you ever read *Gullier's Travels*? This is like the country of the giants, Brobdingnag. I would never have believed . . ." Shaking his head, he walked on.

The blocks cleared and the ground fell suddenly away in a steep descent. "What's this?" she heard him say, more to himself than to her, and he stopped. Before him was the quarry, and below that, reflecting the face of the rock behind, lay the pool she had spoken of, deep green where the last sun fell, black and brooding in the shade.

"Rachel," he called. "Rachel, have you seen this?"

She stood beside him, tucking her hand in his belt.

"Sure," she said, using his own voice. "I was born here, remember?"

"You knew this was here all the time? See how they have cut it? The pale stone beneath? It's like I said. Under the skin is something else. Pink, like flesh. You know those mammoths they found in the ice and the wolves that came and tore away the hide to get at the flesh? After all those years? After hundreds of thousands of years? This was here when there was nothing . . ."

"There are caves," she said. "See the darkest spots? And the green? That's the spring. There's moss and ferns everywhere around there."

She pointed low on the quarry face, almost at the level of the pool.

"It's easy to get to from here. There's the old access road. Right there. That goes around the edge. You don't have to climb. I thought you might . . ."

"I'm going down," he said, scrambling onto level ground. "Quick. It's nearly dark."

He turned and reached for her hand, and she jumped down beside him.

Immediately above the water line of the pool the face of the rock was pitted with hollows and caves, the largest head height, and equally wide.

"I could stay here," he said, walking in and reaching up to touch the roof. "It's dry. And there's stacks of room. I could leave the bike up there, in those Gulliver rocks. Then even if the Angel did come looking, he would never find it. I could spread out here and work forever."

Rachel was watching from the cave entrance, laughing. "You remind me of one of those women in a house and garden magazine. When she sees her new house for the first time, she goes around looking at everything, saying 'Oh, wonderful! Oh, lovely!' Anyway, come and see the spring. I have to go."

"You could stay," he said. "Your dad's out on the boat, isn't he?"

He went to hold her, but she was too fast for him, ducking away.

"No," she said. "Come on. I want to go. It's late. See, there's your spring."

He looked in the direction that she pointed. Below them, accessible by easy stages, was the pool, yet in one place only, a little above the water, the raw edge of the cut stone was obscured by foliage.

"See," she said, standing away as much to let him see as to avoid his reach. "Running water at your door."

His face lit with delight, and he scrambled down. From beneath a rocky overhang, its source lost in darkness, a stream of clear water tumbled to the pool below. Every rock and crevice was thick with green: ferns sprouted, some fine and soft, some sharp and bristling, but all lush and sparkling with moisture. Higher, where they might catch the sun, clumps of amethyst rock orchids bloomed and wood violets trailed slender stems all over, as if to cover what little stone remained.

But when Sam looked back toward where Rachel had been standing, he could not see her. He got up, lifting himself onto the ledge above the spring. She was on the access road, almost at the Gulliver rocks. He called, "Rachel, wait. Rachel . . ."

"You'll be all right," she answered. "See you in the

morning," and her voice echoed in the quarry long
after she had gone.

VI

When Rachel and Sam left, Sarah had gone to her
room, taken up her position in her chair, and sat, gazing out to sea. And so she remained, lost in thought,
until the first breath of night wind stirred the grasses
of the dunes. *Well,* she thought, *that's that. She was the
best friend I'm ever likely to have. Now there's only me, and
Mum, and* . . . She pushed her hair out of her face and
got up, wagging a finger at her reflection, faintly visible in the window. *But there will be no more feeling sorry
for yourself either. Now get out and do something.*

She took her gingham dress from a cupboard and
tossed it over the back of her chair. She raised the lid
of the sea locker at the foot of her bed, rummaged
through its contents, and removed a box. She checked
the label. *Van Dorn's. The Mail Order Specialists.* She
opened it and placed a pair of black flat-heeled patent-
leather shoes on the rug. From the top of her dresser,
she took a brush and comb, from a drawer beneath,
fresh underclothes.

"Now," she said aloud. "A bath."

When she had dried and powdered herself and
brushed out her hair, holding it in place with clips like

butterflies—*horrible,* she thought—she pulled the dress on and put herself through the contortions required to button and bow it—mumbling and muttering "straitjacket" and similar terms of loathing. Then, stepping into her shoes, she went out to her mother, on the chair on the verandah.

"Mum," she said, "I have to go out. I'll be gone about an hour. I'll get your dinner when I come back. If you're not here, don't expect me to go looking for you. Do you understand? Good. 'Bye."

At the church gate she caught sight of the Angel working in the garden. In all the fuss of the afternoon, she had forgotten him, how Sam had said he was there. She said to herself, *Now, Pollyanna, here is a situation you must deal with,* and hitching up the front of the dress, she opened the gate, calling, "Angel, Angel. Is the Father here?"

He had been digging—turning the soil with a fork—and looked up, surprised.

"What?" he said.

She went toward him, taking care where she stepped among the beds. "I said, is the Father here? Have you seen him?"

In reply he rested his hands on the fork and threw his head back, laughing.

She waited. This was a performance, she knew.

When he had done, he said, "You got the wrong

day. This is Friday. You're two days early for that women's service. You got all dolled up for nothing."

She moved closer, standing directly in front of him.

"There he is," she said, glancing in the direction of the church, and when he turned to see—as she knew he would—she snatched the fork from his grip and he sprang back, his hand at the knife on his belt.

"Now," she said, "I expect an answer."

"He's inside."

"In the church?"

"There." He lifted his hand from the knife and pointed to the back of the church, to the annex where the Father lived. "I just seen him."

Stepping past, she allowed the fork to fall. "Thanks," she said.

He stopped to retrieve it, saying something she did not catch.

"Sorry?" She knew that she was pushing him, and the risks involved. "Sorry? What did you say?"

He straightened up, sneering. "I said, I know what's wrong with you."

"What? Tell me."

"It's Rachel, hey?"

"What's she got . . ."

"Her and that city boy. I seen him come in before. Walking down the track to her place. I seen him go, too, on that bike. He came down to see her, hey? Not you. But he won't stay. No. I showed him my blade. I flashed it for him. He's too gutless to stay here."

He bent to resume digging but looked up and added, "Anyway, go on in. You'll make the Father happy. Specially since you're all done up so pretty."

She turned toward the church. *He's right*, she told herself. *That's the trouble. He's right.*

At the door to the annex, she knocked and stood back. As a child she had been here often enough, playing in the garden, imagining her unicorns and dragons while her mother was inside. But now she waited. She glanced down at her dress, at her shoes. She lifted her hand to her hair to check the clips. She was about to knock again when her shoulder was gripped from behind, and she turned, catching her breath.

"Father."

He stood immediately behind her; she was almost in his arms.

"My, my," he said, appraising her. "Is this our Sarah? Dressed for Sunday? My, my."

"Father, I have come . . ."

"Yes," he said. "I saw. You made quite an entrance. I was in the far corner, gathering fruit." He held out a basket of limes for her to see. "I noticed you come in. And what followed."

Here he leaned forward, intimately.

"You must watch my Angel. Sometimes he guards too well."

She raised her shoulder, and he released his grip.

"However, since you are here, I should take you in."

"Father, I don't need . . ."

He laughed. "Nonsense. Your mother always went in." He reached forward, and the door swung open. "Why shouldn't you?"

"No," she said, dropping her head. "Please. Just for now, could we talk out here?"

He looked over the garden. The Angel had gone. With a smile he took her arm and turned her about.

In the Temple

I

It can't be, Rachel said to herself when she arrived at the jetty the next morning, but as she came closer, there could be no doubt; Sarah was there with her mother—and both were sorting. Sarah looked up and shook her head, meaning "Be quiet," and taking the hint, Rachel pulled down one of her father's catch boxes and got on with the job in silence, knowing that an explanation would come.

Hardly had she finished the first box than Sarah said, "Here. That looks like a heavy one. I'll give you a hand carrying it down."

Rachel looked up and smiled, thinking, *Nicely done, Sarah.*

"Thanks," she said. "There are some decent snapper in there for once. It's about time they had a good catch," and they continued to make conversation until they were halfway down the jetty, when Sarah said, "OK. Stop. Put it down here. Make out you're taking a break."

When this was done and they had arched their backs in a pretense of stretching, she said, "I woke up this morning and Mum was in my room, already in that blue dress."

"I saw," Rachel interrupted. "She hasn't worn that since the day Mum died."

"I know, I know." Sarah touched her lips, again asking for quiet.

"There she was, standing at my window, looking out. I called, 'Mum,' and she turned around. 'I'm going to the jetty,' she said. 'I'll help you sort, while I watch.' 'Watch?' I said. 'Watch for what?' Then she smiled for the first time, see, and she said, 'It's over. You wait and see.' That was it. She got up and got dressed and came down here just like she used to."

"What's over? Didn't she say anything else?"

"Nothing. And you can see that she's all right. Just as well it was a good catch for once and there was plenty to do. I watched her do two boxes before you came down. She never made a mistake. And she's fast."

Rachel looked at the woman sorting and shook her head.

"Sarah, don't leave her now. Go back. I'll get this onto ice."

She reached down to pick up the catch box, but Sarah gripped her wrist, stopping her.

"Wait," she said. "While she's still busy, let me tell you the rest. But you're not going to like it."

"What?"

"I'm cleaning the Father's place. I . . ."

"Sarah, no."

Sarah stepped forward, putting her hand over her friend's mouth. "Shut up. Just this once, shut up."

Rachel pulled away, wiping the salt from her lips with the back of her hand.

"Have you gone mad?" she said. "Have you? Aren't there enough idiots around this place already?"

"Will you let me finish?"

"No. Not if you're going to talk rubbish. Cleaning up after the Father is against everything we believe in. Everything. It's horrible. Or are you joking? You are, aren't you?"

"I'm not. When you left with Sam yesterday, I made a decision. I dressed up and paid the Father a visit. I told him that I couldn't cope. That I believed Mum was sick because of me. That it was a judgment, because of my attitude. I told him that I wanted to make things right, that I didn't want her to die, like your mother."

"Sarah, that's terrible."

"I asked if I could work for him, like Mum did, cleaning, if he would pray for us, Mum and me. I made out that I was on my own. You get the idea?"

Rachel could not look at her.

"Rachel. I want some answers. I spent a week with my mother, and I proved nothing. Well, nothing except this: I can't begin to help her until I know what's going on. Don't go. Give me a chance to finish. I know that you tried to get Sam to look in the lantana, and there are things I wanted to do too. I wanted to get into the Father's place. I have to look at that book. That's why I did it. I have to know whether it's real—if that makes sense—or whether it's only more superstition."

"You think the answer is there?"

"It might be. There are little things, like why he comes whispering to my mother. And why he lied about Hannah. It could mean he's just old and dippy. But there's other things. What about the signs we laughed at? I don't know now. And where are the kids in this town? And what goes on at that men's service every Sunday, with them standing there under that net? Is that religion? No. It's some big secret. Rachel, I want to know what goes on here. That's why I did it. To get close."

"Maybe our mothers got too close."

"We aren't our mothers."

"Are we smarter?"

"We aren't our mothers, that's all I said."

They walked to the depot in silence, carrying the catch box between them, but on their return, Rachel said, "I suppose the Father said yes."

Sarah nodded.

"When will you start?"

"This afternoon, after lunch."

Rachel stopped. "What you said about me getting Sam down to the lantana, well, he apologized for how he talked to me, and I got him to agree. I'm going to show him the place after this. But you'll be going up to clean."

"It's not the end of the world," Sarah whispered, almost on top of her mother. "You look after your Sam, and I'll look after the Father. We're women now. OK?"

II

After the sort, as soon as Sarah and her mother were out of sight, Rachel ran the length of the tea-tree path, emerging at the clearing, panting. Sam was there, looking at his wrist as if he had timed her run.

"The herons told me that you were coming," he said, "or at least one of them did. See?"

She looked up. Circling above was a single bird.

"Over here," he said, pointing to the banksias, "we have a nest. I think that's Mrs. Heron flying around, doing guard duty, and Mr. Heron is on the eggs."

She pushed him away. "How would you know?" she said. "Or are you so smart that you can tell the sex of birds?"

"Naturally. And fish. And snakes. Can't all us Abos?"

"You," she said, laughing. "You would be the least likely Aborigine in this country. Sorry to disillusion you but . . ."

He walked with her toward the bank of the lagoon.

"That's not true," he said. "When I swam in here the other day, it was like I'd done it all my life. Every day of my life. That's what made things so hard going up to that church straight after. And last night when you showed me the core . . ."

"Well?"

"When you were gone, I sat there outside the cave and I looked out across the pool, down this way—you can't see the sheds or those Gulliver rocks, they're all hidden by the bush—and I was thinking that maybe my mother was from this tribe. Part of this country. I felt at home. Like I belonged."

"Was it all right up there? Did you get settled?"

"Yes, but no thanks to you, taking off like you did."

The heron came down, gliding low over the water and, with a brief flutter of wings, settled to watch from a stump among the mangroves.

"Sure," he went on. "I slept all right. But being down here makes me think. It's like there are things that I know because I feel them. You could call that intuition. I feel at home here, near the lagoon and that mountain."

He looked back toward the core.

"See how it stands there, saying 'I'm here.' But really it says nothing. I could dig around this place all my life and prove that Aborigines lived here, and how they lived, but I would never know what tribe exactly. I couldn't name them as a people. And I can't prove that my mother had anything to do with them. Not with anthropology anyway. Not with science."

He was silent, looking out across the water.

"What?" she said. "Say what you mean."

"It's that Father. He must know more than he's saying if he's been here all those years. And another thing. I can't understand how he got to be so strong. What his hold over everyone is. If it's like you say, he's the ruler here. A sort of god."

He shrugged and sighed. "Don't worry. Forget it. How about these spats? Aren't they neat?"

He suddenly waddled off across the clearing in a parody of Charlie Chaplin, his mud-caked feet kicking up the sand as he moved.

"I thought you'd finished in the mud," she said, laughing. "I thought you would be working up here. Checking on the extent . . ."

He stopped and turned to face her.

"What you really mean is, 'Oh, Sam, you promised that you would go into the scratchy, spooky lantana with me.' I'm right, aren't I? You think that you can fool me into doing whatever you want."

"That's not true. I was only asking because . . ."

"Don't worry. I'd go into the lantana with you anytime."

"Good," she said, ignoring his nonsense. "Where's your gear?"

"Over by my old camp."

"Well, get it out of sight. Then we'll go back up into the tea trees and around through the cemetery. That way."

"I know," he said. "I made it down from the core this morning, all by myself, remember?"

III

She turned off the path to enter the cemetery from the seaward side. He was behind her.

"Look," he said, "you can see the core better from here, without the trees in the way."

He took her shoulder, turning her slightly, but she shrugged him off.

"Sam, I know where the core is, and what it looks like. I've lived under its shadow all my life. Besides, that's the back of the lantana over there, on the other side." She indicated an outcrop of thicker scrub. "That's what I wanted you to see."

He nodded, looking about. Scattered through the long, dry grass were weathered headstones. All were of basalt, some chipped, some cracked, some bleached, some stained, some leaning one way, some another.

"Did you know of any of these people?" he said, kneeling to inspect the stone nearest to him. " 'Anna, Beloved Wife of Thomas'?"

He turned to another before she could answer. "Or 'Sadly Missed, Our Darling Son Jonas, Now With the Angels'? Or 'Resting in the Bosom of the Deep, My Husband, Our Father, Zachariah Humm . . .' I can't read the rest."

When there was no response, he glanced up.

"No. I didn't know them," she said, her voice matter-of-fact. "Although I knew most of their families. If you checked the dates, you would see they go back a long way. They've been dead a long time. But I don't see how that gives you the right to make fun of them, now they're gone."

"It was just a joke," he said, standing. "Places like this are amazing. Did you know that burial sites and rubbish dumps provide more information about cultures than anywhere else? You see these headstones? I could take an inventory here and make all sorts of hypotheses regarding this community: date of settlement, nationality of original settlers—I can see names here from all over Europe. I might even find trends in that pattern—like the Italian names—then maybe average age at death, common causes of death—if the headstones state them; then of course, if you could dig them up, the bodies would . . ."

"This is the oldest part of the cemetery," she interrupted. "It began over by the lantana, where I was taking you, and spread around this way. All that part is new—the Steele boys I told you about are over there. So is my mother. . . ."

At once he realized what he had said.

"Rachel. I'm sorry. Honestly, I didn't mean to hurt you. I . . ."

"You didn't."

She looked away, pointing inland, in the direction of the core, where the entrance plinths were visible above the headstones. "Those were going to be gates, or so someone told me once. But they were never finished. Anyway, there isn't even a fence."

"What is there to keep out?"

"Nothing," she said, then added, under her breath, "Or in."

"Do you come down here very much? I mean, because of your mother?"

"In the mornings, after the sort. But sometimes I think there's no point. There's no headstone on her grave, or anything like that. There's no special place marked, not like these old ones. No stone book with her name carved on it. They used the quarry stone once, but not anymore. So many have died. Her grave is just piled-up dirt."

"Everyone should have some special place. It would be terrible if it ended up being your grave."

"I don't know if there was anywhere special for Mum. When I was old enough to know her properly, she was gone. I never knew things like that about her. I never had the chance."

She had been staring in the direction of the plinths and now turned toward him.

"Do you have a place?"

"Once I would have said my room back at the home. I was born there, so Hibbert says. But now, like I was saying, I'd like to spend some time around the core, working there, the same as I have been near the lagoon. My people would have known that place. Those caves and that pool. All round here is special. What about you?"

"Anywhere along that tea-tree path. I've liked it since I was little. Sarah would be in her room reading, but I would be off down there. Then you turned up, almost in the same place."

"Does that make it special?"

"What?"

"That I was there?"

"Yes."

"And did you ever see anyone else there?"

"What?"

"Did you ever meet anyone else there. You know. Alone."

They talked over the graves, making no attempt to move.

"There never was anyone else. Only Sarah. All that about the Angel and him being arranged for me, well, that's been said since I was a child. But never by me or my parents. Only ever by him, and his papa. Or the Father."

"Not his mother?"

She shook her head. "That's her. About six or eight over."

She walked a little toward the plinths, stopping above a grave marked by a carved scroll.

"Maria Rossellini. My mother showed me where she was buried years ago. She died in childbirth."

"Having Angel?"

"No. Not him. A baby girl. She's in there too, with her mother. She was never named. That was the same time Sarah and I were born. She would have been the same age as us if she had lived. The Angel is older."

"Then things might be different. He might have treated you differently if he had a sister."

She laughed, and he looked at her, surprised.

"What?" he said. "How come *you're* allowed to laugh?"

"Because of you. Thinking that a woman could make any difference around here. That she could make a change."

"Well? Couldn't she? One like you?"

She shook her head.

"Come on. I have to show you this place, then get home to do Dad's lunch. Does that answer your question?"

She led him through the headstones toward the lantana. As they walked, she said, "You see, these are very old. Everything is worn away. Names. Dates. That stone *is* quite soft really."

"It seems funny, all the trouble people go to, but after a few years it all comes down to nothing ."

"People remember," she said.

"Sure, but for how long? Can you tell me who any of these people are? Their names?"

"Someone might know."

He laughed. "Rachel, we start off without names and end up without names. That's what it comes down to."

She stopped at the edge of the lantana.

"You're a strange person," she said. "All this about wanting to know who you are, and your people, and now you tell me it doesn't even matter. So what's the point? Why bother about anything?"

"You don't understand . . ."

She raised her hand, cutting him off. "And I don't want to. Not now. We're here now, and I want you to have a look. We wind around for a while. This is a labyrinth."

"Is there a Minotaur?"

"I've only been here once, so if I get lost, don't yell at me. And no more smart remarks. OK?"

She was swallowed up by the lantana.

"Wait," he said, "wait."

Up ahead he heard her laugh. "I told you. You have to stay near me."

"A pleasure," he said.

Then there was silence. It was almost noon. There was no breeze, and the lantana was close; coarse stems rubbed one on the other, and the odor of the leaves was strong.

"It's hot," he whispered.

"Not far," she replied.

"It scratches," he whispered.

Soon, she thought, *it must be soon or else he will go back. Let it be soon.*

"Rachel . . ."

Then she was through and Sam behind her. It was exactly as she remembered.

"There," she said. "I told you."

He went straight to the center of the clearing, turning a full circle, taking in where he was.

"This isn't natural," he said. "It couldn't be. It's too . . ."

"Too circular?"

"Too constructed. Like a nest, a giant bird's nest. Like the one in Sinbad."

Before she could warn him, he dropped to his knees.

"Ow," he said. "That hurt. What the hell . . . ?"

"It's those stones. I told you. They're just under the surface. Look."

She knelt beside him, scooping up the sand and tossing it to one side.

"There. See? And here. All over."

He followed suit, tunneling the sand between his legs, until he had cleared a small depression, its base dimpled with the tops of the round stones.

"Curiouser and curiouser," he mumbled. "And they're packed tight."

"I told you that. I said Mrs. Goodwin broke her nails lifting them."

"She lifted them?"

"No. But she tried."

"The sand is the trouble too. Falling back into the hole. Here. You hold it back. Yes. Now I can get to these . . ."

He gripped a stone with both hands, working it backward and forward until it was loose. "There. Now. It's coming out. I've got it." And he tumbled backward, still clasping the stone.

Immediately she put her hand into the cavity. "It's hard at the bottom. It's metal."

No more was said. Working together, they removed another, then another, until beside each was a pile of stones.

"Let me try again," she said.

Once more she cleared the layer of fallen sand.

"There. It's corrugated. That's what it is. I bet it's a sheet of tin."

"Try elsewhere," he said, moving toward the point where they had come in. "You try there. I'll do here."

In minutes they had uncovered the same configuration: sand, then stone, then metal.

"That's why nothing grows here," he said. "It's not only the rocks. There must be sheets of tin under the whole area."

"A layer of rock, then a layer of tin. I bet."

He could not understand. "Sure," he said, "but what for? Unless it's covering something."

"Why would you go to all that trouble? What would you have to cover?"

"A well. An old well drop." He looked at her, waiting for her approval.

She shook her head. "Why would Mrs. Goodwin want to dig that up?"

"You keep saying that. Mrs. Goodwin is . . ." He stopped. "Mrs. Goodwin mightn't have been digging anything up. She might have been playing sand castles."

"No," she said. "She's not crazy. And it's too big for a well, too wide."

"It might be a mine shaft."

"A mine shaft? Here? Mining what?"

He did not answer. He got up and went to the mouth of the tunnel.

"Is this where you came in with Sarah? Through here?"

"Yes," she said, moving closer.

"It looks like an animal track or something."

"What animals?"

"Dogs?"

"Not likely. There's no pets in New Canaan."

"Then native animals. A wallaby, or something."

"A wallaby?" She bent down, peering into the tunnel, then looked back. "A wallaby hopped in and made this? Is that what you're saying?"

"It might have."

"You don't know much about wallabies, do you?" she said, and went to the center of the clearing.

The heat was intense. He leaned forward, pulling his T-shirt over his head.

She dropped to her knees in the sand. "Well, can we see what's under the tin then?"

He looked at her. "Why? What would that prove? This is no Aboriginal site. I don't have to go to the university to work that out. This has got nothing to do with the midden. So why?"

"I told you. A thousand times. Because . . ."

"Because Mrs. Goodwin was digging here. OK. If it makes you happy. But I'm lifting one sheet. That's all."

"No," she said, "we're both lifting one sheet. Right here, where we started."

"What about your father's corned beef sandwich? Shouldn't you . . . ?"

"He can wait five minutes. Come on."

She began shifting the sand, tossing it in handfuls to the perimeter. He spread his shirt on the foliage and knelt opposite her.

"I could go back and get my spade and my pick. It would make this faster. You would save your nails."

She held up her hand. The fingernails were dull and blunt. "I work at the jetty," she said, "not some swanky salon."

He said no more.

When they had cleared a patch a yard across, she said, "The sheets run your way," and they changed positions to dig again, until a length of heavily corroded roofing tin was exposed.

"Can we get under it?" Rachel said. "Can we lift it straight out?"

Sam nodded, the sweat dripping from his forehead to splatter on the tin.

"Just give me . . ." he began, but she had mistaken his cue. He was not ready. The corner of the tin nearest his right hand slashed across his fingers, and with a cry he sprang back, holding his hand high, shaking it.

"What is it?" she said, dropping the sheet and stumbling forward. "What did I do?"

"My finger's cut. It's all right. I won't die."

She reached out to be shown, but he turned away. "Show me."

He held his hand out. On the index finger she saw blood oozing from a flap of skin.

"I'm sorry," she said. "I should have waited. I should . . ."

He stepped aside, not wanting to be fussed over. "Can we stop now?" he said. "I've had enough."

"Then leave it. I'll do it myself. It doesn't matter."

"It does matter. You want to."

He knelt again, lifting his end of the sheet, waiting for her to return and take hers. When she was ready, he said, "On three. One, two, three."

The sheet bowed in the middle, almost collapsing under its own weight. They stepped to one side, dropped it, then turned to see. Beneath was sand, compressed in the corrugated pattern of the tin, but emerging from it, like worms, were loops of black rope, as thick as fingers.

"What the hell?"

"That's an old net," she said. "An old tarred net. Why would that . . .?"

"A bad catch? Could they have buried a bad catch?"

She was on her knees, leaning forward. "How do you mean, a bad catch?"

He dropped down beside her. "I don't know. Like a net full of rotten fish. Or polluted fish. I wouldn't know."

She shook her head. "Anything bad is dumped at sea. Even our household rubbish."

"What about a whale? A beached whale?"

"Why bother?"

"To stop the stink."

"What? Drag it all the way up here and cover it in tin and rocks? She was probing in the sand with her fingers, tugging at the loops of the net. "No," she said. "It's not that. This is really strange. This was a good net. There's a lot of time and money gone into making this. It was someone's good net. They don't throw these away down here."

"What about a horse? Or a big animal like that? Killed up on the road?"

She lifted her head. "There's something up, isn't there? Something you don't want to know."

He forced a laugh. "Don't be silly. Like what? What wouldn't I want to know?"

She looked back at the pit. "Nothing."

As if to prove her wrong, he grabbed a hank of rope and pulled it toward him. It gave a little, lifting and cracking the tightly packed sand around it. He pulled again. It gave a little more, revealing the webbing of the net. Saying nothing, she crawled around beside him. The next time they pulled together. The net came away easily, then stopped abruptly.

"It's caught on something," she said. "We would have to lift more."

He did not reply. Tangled in the newly revealed webbing was a piece of rotten cloth: black or dark blue. He reached forward with both hands to disentangle it, grunting with the effort, then held it up, shaking it out.

"A vest," he said. "A man's vest." She reached for something else, a belt, and as she withdrew it, a boot appeared. "All clothes," she said.

Sam inched forward, carefully lifting the collapsed webbing. He slipped his fingers beneath.

"What?" Rachel said, trying to see. He placed an object in the palm of his hand and extended it to her.

"A bit of china? A cup handle?" He shook his head. "It's a bone. It's a finger bone. I know it. There's a body . . ."

There came a long sigh. The lantana stirred and rustled. The earth had trembled and was still.

"Sam," she said, her eyes huge with fear.

The bone had dropped from his hand. His palms were pressed flat on the sand. He was staring toward the core.

"Sam, what is it?"

He waited, as if to be sure the threat had passed, then he looked back to her. "The ground shook, like an earth tremor."

She got up at once. "I'm going home," she said. "Leave this. Cover it up."

He went after her, catching her hand.

"Rachel, listen."

She pulled away from him, then stopped, waiting.

"Someone is buried here. All tangled up in that net. I'm sure of it. We can't just leave."

She was desperate to go. She rubbed her hands together. She touched her face, her hair.

"I have to go," she said. "This is awful. All of it. I'm sorry that I started it."

"Who started it?"

He grabbed her shoulders, forcing her to be still. "Not you. Whoever put that thing in that hole started it. Not you. You hear? You hear? But you can finish it. That's what you wanted. Remember? That's what this was all about. Wanting to know. Well?"

She pushed at him, and he stumbled back.

"All right," she said. "All right. You don't have to break my arms. Let's finish it, then. But not now. I can't do it now. Not with all that's happened. I don't like it, any of it. Later, later today. OK?"

He had moved around the clearing. He bent to pick up the vest and belt and boot. He dropped them back into the pit, dragging the tin over the hole. He searched the sand, found the bone, and put it in the pocket of his shorts. He mopped his face with his T-shirt, then draped it around his shoulders. Finally he said, "No. Not today. Tomorrow."

"Why? Why wait that long?"

"Tomorrow morning. Sunday. When old Gray Eye

is at his women's service. When your men are sleeping off their Saturday night grog."

"And me? If I'm not there, he will come looking."

"Then be there. Let me do this. Now, let's go. Just act like everything is normal."

As he spoke, the earth shook again.

This was the sixth sign.

IV

After lunch Sarah said to Joseph, "I have to go out. Keep your eye on Mum. I'll be back before you go down to the Rest."

But as she walked in the lane, a feeling of uncertainty came over her and she stopped to look back. Nothing. She retraced her steps. There was Joseph on the verandah and her mother beside him. *You do imagine things,* she said to herself.

At the Father's annex she knocked, and presently the door swung open and he was there, smiling his smile.

"Well," he said, "if it isn't our Sarah—and in her overalls, ready to work."

She stepped in, and the door closed.

After the midday brilliance of the garden, she could barely see. The whitewashed glass of a single window shed a sickly light. She stood awkwardly, adjusting to the gloom.

"I will make tea," he said. "Then we will talk. Here, you sit down."

In front of her was a pine table with two chairs. She sat without a word, keeping her hands in her lap. While he fussed with a kettle, she looked about, thinking, *I am alone with him, in his place, on his terms,* and she calculated methods of escape.

The annex was an extension of the back of the church. It could be entered from the garden, as she had done, or through the church itself by means of a curtained archway, secured by a door, behind the altar. The Father was very taken with making theatrical entrances through this arch, particularly at the service of women.

Sarah could see the curtain now, drab and limp in the gloom at the rear of the annex.

"Yes, please," she answered when he asked about sugar, but as he reached high for the canister, she looked again.

"That is my reading room, or the library, as I call it," he said without turning. "Behind you, in the alcove, is my bed." He glanced back at her, and she dropped her eyes.

When the tea was ready, he set it in front of her.

"This is nice. It's so rarely that I have visitors. Except my Angel, of course, and he is hardly a visitor."

He chuckled, taking his place opposite her, pouring her tea.

"It seems that I am always doing the visiting myself."

The cup and saucer were very fine, the china white and light as shell, the handle so dainty she was afraid it would snap. "Father," she said, seeing there was only one cup. "Aren't you having any?"

"No," he answered. "I have made two visits this morning and had tea twice. And cake."

She placed the cup carefully on its saucer. "If you visit often," she said, "you need a very small cup to carry with you. My mother has one. It is called a conversation cup. It holds no more than a thimble. It was her mother's."

"It was her grandmother's," he said.

She lifted her cup and sipped.

He placed his elbows on the table, resting his chin on his interlocked fingers. *He looks at me as if I am an insect,* she thought.

And when she had put the cup down, conscious of the brown tea ring that had formed in the saucer, he said, "Finish your tea—it is imported, English. There is plenty of time."

"No, Father," she said, "I should begin. I left my mother with the men, and they will be going to the Fisherman's Rest. It's Saturday."

"Ah." He raised his hands, bringing them together

at his lips. "How foolish of me. Here I was thinking we could sit and talk. But these fishermen are
the same the world over, and have been since the
beginning."

Leaning forward, he whispered, "They all like their
drink."

She smiled and nodded.

"Well," he said, pushing back his chair, "let us begin.
You might start with that cup. Bring it with you."

She followed him to a porcelain sink beneath the
window.

"Rinse it here," he said, "and leave it to dry. Later,
you will wipe this area down. All cleaning aids are in
here." He opened a tall cupboard, but in the darkness
she could see nothing.

"Father," she said, "there is so little light. I doubt
that I will see where to clean."

"You will grow used to it. There can be too much
light. Too much . . ."

He tapped his foot on the stone floor. "This can be
mopped one week, scrubbed the next. You will leave
the bedroom. Someone else attends to that."

"The bathroom?" she said, looking.

He did not answer, and she followed him to the
doorway of his library. Beneath the curtain on the far
wall shone a sliver of light.

"On the other side is the church," he said.

He crossed the darkness like a ghost, and without
so much as the click of a switch, there was light.

Two orbs lit the room; the larger and brighter shone overhead; the smaller and softer glowed low in the dark.

"Father . . ." But as she spoke, he moved again, and before her there appeared a globe, a marvelous thing, spinning slowly and silently at his touch, its seas of blue, its continents of green, its islands of gold, and as it turned, the books that lined the darkness were touched with light.

Sarah could not resist. She reached up and removed a volume. On the spine, embossed in gold, was the title: *A Complete Collection of Voyages and Travels.* Before he could prevent her, she had opened it, holding it to the light, and on the flyleaf, written by hand in faded purple, were the words *Ex Libris Liberty.* Immediately she remembered: "Wonderful books, bound in leather and trimmed in gold: books of the sea, of Antipodean lands, of the stars and planets and the firmament beyond; books of poetry and people." These were the books lost from the *Liberty.* They belonged in her room.

The Father's hands closed over hers, clapping the book shut.

She sprang back, startled.

"Father . . ." she began.

He turned to replace the volume. "Don't read," he said. "Only dust, as the other women do."

But as he spoke, she felt the floor beneath her tremble, and a light wind, no more than a breath, lifted the dividing curtain to brush the globe. From somewhere came the faintest tinkle of glass.

"Father . . ."

"It was a gust off the sea."

"That was more than the wind. That was the ground. It moved. I'm certain."

He placed his hands on the globe and lifted his head, sensing, like an animal. "Your imagination," he said, and pulling aside the curtain, he passed through the doorway into the church.

She followed, not knowing what else to do.

When they stood beside the altar, he said, "Touch nothing here. Leave the altar alone. Under no circumstances touch the icon. The Angel will polish that. But here"—and he moved into the body of the church— "you will dust all seats and do the floors as in the annex, mopped one week, scrubbed the next. Places to watch . . ."

He led her down the aisle, showing her where sand drifted in, where there might be cobwebs. Outside, in the porch, the doormat was to be shaken.

"Here is the key," he said, lifting the mat, to show it nestled beneath. She stared. *All these years. All his secrecy. And he keeps the key beneath the mat?*

Then he took her back, and at the altar he said, "I will leave you now. You will begin in here."

She did not move.

"Is something wrong?" he said.

"Is that all?"

He raised his eyebrows. "You want more?"

She said nothing.

He came closer to her. "Later," he said. "You are too soon." Smiling, he reached for the curtain.

Then the earth shook. The porch door slammed shut and burst open. Pews lifted and thumped. Walls warped and groaned. The moaning of the wind was everywhere. Just as suddenly it stopped.

She had fallen by the altar.

He was on his knees in the archway, the curtain torn away and gripped in his hands.

Now pieces fell from the fisherman's window. The figures in the net. They shattered on the stone floor, on the altar.

She made no attempt to speak but scrambled to her knees, thinking, *Go . . . Get out . . . There is danger . . .* The archway behind him was nearest. She scrambled past, half-crouching, and stumbled into the library. The orb lights were out. *Go, go,* was all she could think, yet there was the globe shining bright as day, and there was a door where there had been darkness.

She hesitated and looked back. From the church, nothing, not a sound or movement. *Here?* she thought. *Could it be in here?* She pushed the door, and the light increased. She pushed again, peering in.

Set high in the wall was a window and, on a stand beneath, its pages bright and drenched in light, lay an open book.

"So," she said softly and pulled the door shut.

Massacre of the Innocents

The morning sun woke Sam, penetrating his place in the mountain, and he wandered out to look over the bush toward the lagoon. He sighed, thinking what had to be done, of the dig in the lantana. *Not yet,* he thought. *Soon.*

He took his towel and clambered down the rocks toward the spring, but immediately he reached it, he stopped, astounded. Every green fern of the previous day, and every flower, hung yellow-brown and wilted; the water itself ran red, and reaching forward, he felt its heat. He turned to the pool; steamy wisps of vapor drifted on its surface. When he lifted his head, the sharp odor of gas filled his nostrils.

This is volcanic, he thought, *a result of that tremor.* He sat for a time, watching the movement of water, until his vision blurred and he felt strange . . . disoriented, and assumed it was the gas.

Later he gathered his gear and made his way down to the cemetery. He stepped carefully among the unmarked graves, then entered the lantana.

The site was very hot. The white sand reflected the sun, and the thickness of the foliage blocked any breeze off the lagoon. *There were black stones,* he thought, *just a little beneath, absorbing heat. Sheets of tin too.*

It was not difficult to ascertain the parameter of the dig; the hedgelike wall of the lantana clearly delineated the circular site. Still, he remembered his training and sketched the area on graph paper, measuring the diameter of the clearing with a tape. He gathered flowers and foliage from the lantana, placing both in a clear plastic envelope and sealing it. He stapled the envelope to his sketch, shading the area covered by the thicket, and labeled it *Lantana Species.*

Working clockwise, he paced the circumference of the clearing, stopping every yard to prod the sand gently with his spade, checking for the point of resistance which told where rocks or tin lay beneath or, if the spade penetrated deeper, where there was nothing, only sand.

These soundings he recorded.

Now he was ready. He ignored the makeshift attempt

of the previous day, reasoning that three wedge-shaped digs, converging on the center, would be enough to evaluate the site—as well as saving time; the service of women would not last all morning.

He began at the edge directly opposite his point of entry. He cleared the surface sand with the shovel; then, when the layer of black rocks was exposed, he worked with a trowel and his hands, clearing what remained with a brush. He recorded the size and relative position of each rock, then removed it. He collected the sand from the sheet of tin that lay beneath, brushing it into a paper cone, like a dustpan, checking its content and putting it aside.

The first sheet ran at an angle to his wedge. *Then I change,* he thought, and following the pattern of corrugations, he widened the dig to allow the sheet to be raised in one piece and adjusted his records accordingly.

When the sheet was completely cleared, he crouched near the center of the site and reached into the trench. The edges of the tin were rusted and jagged. He made certain of his grip; the cut on his finger was still open and throbbing. He pulled, dragging backward, until the entire sheet had been withdrawn; then he looked. There were the telltale loops of black rope. He could grab any one of these and pull the whole thing out. Then he would know. "Remember your method," he said aloud, and wiping the sweat from his forehead, he returned to his gear. He drank water from a bottle, then rummaged through his bag for the vegetable strainer he used as a sieve. With this in one hand and his trowel in the other, he knelt at the edge of the trench, scooping or scraping the sand from the webbing of the net, then sifting and examining each load before discarding it.

When the heat grew unbearable and every part of him cried out to stop, he repeated, "Remember your method," and kept on, until the trowel nudged something dense, not the net, softer, and he found his brush and cleared away the clinging sand, and there was cloth, multicolored, and carefully, gripping it between his thumb and finger, he pulled it free. It was a shirt, rolled in a ball, and rotten, but its floral print was clear enough. *This could be a woman's,* he thought. When he had sealed this in a bag and set it aside, he picked up the trowel to resume, but there in the hole, with the drying sand trickling down, were bones. He craned forward. He had uncovered a human foot. With his fingers he worked back toward the ankle, and when he had reached the primary bones of the leg, he knew that this was too much for him, too big. *A camera,* he thought, *I need a camera,* but he recorded the find as best he could, covered the hole with tin, and anchored it with rocks. *Until later,* he thought. *I'll come back later.*

He stopped to drink, then chose the next site, blocking out the wedge and clearing it as he'd done before. He worked faster, as much through fear as lack of time, and when he had removed the tin and reached the tangle of rope, he said to himself, *Slow down, Sam. Slow down.* In this place the net was bunched tightly. He rocked back on his haunches, wiping away sweat with his forearm, thinking, *I could get under it and pull the lot out. Pull it out in one go. I could.* But as before, he recorded the find, replaced the tin, anchored it with rocks, and moved on.

In the third trench the net was loose, its webbing close to the surface. He sifted the top sand, stopping often to drink or wipe his face. He felt sick. Giddy with the heat, the excitement. Who could he tell? Someone. Rachel should know. Sarah too. He could call Jordy. He could say, "Come down. There are human skeletons, I think." Whatever he did, he must do properly. He would be judged by what he did. His lecturers could see this. Or the police, if it was murder. . . .

Protruding from the net were the bones of a hand, and beneath this, another, the bones frail, separated only by sand. His graph paper was buried. He kept no record. He lifted the net, and the bones slid aside. Now there was fabric, shreds of cotton. And beneath that, a rib cage, supported, it seemed, by the sand beneath. He dusted with his brush, his sweat dripping on the bones. He cleared the forearm to the elbow, the collarbone, the shoulder blade, he gouged deeper for

the neck—*fallen back,* he thought, *flopped back in death.*
His fingers discovered the chin and traced the line of
the jaw until he could bear it no longer and dug in,
cupping the skull in his hands, feeling his fingertips
touch behind. He pulled it free, in one piece, and
there it was, grinning at him, ridiculous, its eyes filled
with sand—*like a mask at a party,* he thought, *like a
party joke*—until the jaw twisted and fell. He looked
down, and there directly below was another, smaller,
white and smooth as china, on its side this time, in
profile, but clear of sand since it had been covered by
the other, protected by it. He put the first aside and
reached down to touch, but as he did, there was
movement—some sudden shift of sand or release of
fetid air—and the skull tilted and rolled, catching his
finger, his flap of skin. He pulled back with a cry, then
looked again, seeing the baby size of it. He touched its
crushed and splintered bone. His blood smeared on
its china whiteness.

Sensing he was falling, he raised himself to cry out,
yet nothing came: no voice, no name. He fell forward
into the pit, surrendering to darkness.

II

From the darkness came the sound of many voices,
shrieking and crying and moaning, and there were
limbs without bodies, crawling one on the other, rub-

bing one against the other, and hands, without limbs, reaching and grasping and clawing, and one rose up and opened before his face, its fingers flames, and in its palm was a single eye, and the eye was sightless, and cold as a dead moon, yet turning this way and that, ever watching, ever searching, seeing nothing, except him, only him.

When he opened his eyes, gasping, he was lying in the cave, and the girls were there, somewhere, he could hear them talking, and reassured, he slept.

The next time there was no one, only a wet cloth on his forehead. He lifted his hand to touch it, then drifted away.

When he heard the voices again, he sat up and called out. The girls came in at once. Rachel knelt beside him, using the cloth to push back his damp hair. Sarah stood at his feet.

"How long have I been here?" he said.

"Since midday."

"What time is it now?"

"About three."

"I was in the lantana. I felt sick."

"We found you down there. The two of us. After the service."

"Yes," Sarah said, sitting near Rachel. "And thanks to you my Sunday dress is ruined. There's little bits of it all through the bush."

"So now she's happy."

He looked from one to the other, not understanding. "Did you really find me there?"

They nodded. "And we brought you back here."

"Those tremors, have there been any more?"

"Nothing," Sarah said. "But I was in the church when they came."

Rachel shook her head, to keep her quiet. "We did the lunches and dinners, then came back. It's Sunday, remember."

He glanced toward the entrance. "You got me all the way up here?"

"You could walk. But you were delirious. You talked a lot of rubbish."

He reached up and took the cloth from her hand.

"I'm OK now. But down there was terrible. My notes? Did you find my notes?"

"Sarah got them. And the clothes in the bags. We carried them up when you were asleep."

"Did you look? Did you see what was there? Under the tin?"

"Not at first," Sarah said. "We were too busy helping you. But when we went back, then we looked. We saw everything."

"Well?" he said. "Who are they? Those people down there?"

When neither girl spoke, he sat forward, searching their faces. "Didn't you see? The bones? Those skulls? The little one? That was a kid's head. Don't you understand?"

The girls looked at each other. He sensed their silent

communication, the years of knowing that had been before him.

Sarah said, "We saw. We said that."

He sighed and dropped his head in his hands. He tried again. "OK. Sorry. I'm still a bit woozy. I'm saying, do you understand what I found down there? It's murder. That's what. Mass murder."

"You weren't the only one who found them."

"There's us, and my mother too, remember. She was the first one, trying to shift those stones."

"Who cares who found them? What difference does it make?"

Again they looked at each other.

"You need to get out," Rachel said. "The air in here is foul. Some sort of gas."

She motioned to Sarah to help, but when they attempted to lift him, he laughed.

"I'm not dying. It was just a bit of heat stroke or something. Come on."

He got up and, keeping his head low, moved to the entrance of the cave, where he stood straight, rubbing his eyes, his neck and shoulders. Rachel followed with his sleeping bag, folding it into a cushion.

"There," she said, dropping it against the outside wall. "Sit on that. The air is a bit fresher out here."

Sarah handed him one of his enamel cups, filled with water.

He looked at it doubtfully.

"Don't worry," she said. "It's from your own supply. I saw what happened at the spring. That water is foul too."

"It was those tremors," he said. "They disturbed something, right down beneath this rock." He drank deeply. When he had finished, he looked up, refreshed.

Rachel sat on the ledge opposite him.

"Sam," she said, "we talked all afternoon, Sarah and me. We haven't done that for a long time. And there are things that you should know . . ."

She turned toward Sarah, leaning against the face of the rock, staring down over the bush.

"Sarah, you say, you can tell it better."

Sarah nodded, happy to speak. "When we see a net, like that one down there in the lantana, we know that's a very good net. There's a lot of time gone into making that. People don't go around burying nets like that. They use them."

"Sure, someone used it," he said. "It's got bodies in it."

She took no notice.

"That net down there, that's a Rossellini net. Only the Rossellinis knot rope like that. Always have done, since the . . ."

He shook his head with impatience.

"This is ridiculous. We should be getting the police in here, not sitting around talking."

"Let Sarah finish," Rachel said. "You need to listen."

He leaned back against the rock, drawing his legs up in front.

"All right, I'm listening. But not for long."

"We talked about this all afternoon. We tried to reason it out. For a start, there has always been a thing here about nets. The Father would say how the powers of darkness had a net that would come down for us. We were told that from when we were babies. We were told that the Evil One walked the paths, looking. And the Father would point to the window, the fisherman's window, and there were the sinners, caught, wriggling in his net. But somehow it was all mixed up. From the beginning . . . Then there's the men's service, every Sunday, going on right now. It's held under a net—strung out, high over the jetty. You see? There's something. Like when the Steele boys were drowned and got washed up in a net. Everyone said that was a sign. And then there was my mother. She might be sick, but she knew what was under those rocks. Rachel heard her. Go on, Rachel, let him think that you're mad too."

"The morning we found Mrs. Goodwin in the lantana, when Sarah was trying to get her dressed, she was saying over and over, 'They're all under here. Under the rocks.' She said, 'Eva,' my mother's name, and, 'They're right where they put them,' or something like that."

"So this afternoon, when you were sick, we sat out here and tried to work out who 'they' were."

"Both the ones who were buried and the ones who buried them there."

"Whoever did it has to be local. Because of the net."

"We tried to remember who had gone missing around here since we were kids. We know all the people in this place, and most of the people in that cemetery. Going right back."

"But there was no one. All the people we can remember dying were buried properly, and no one has moved away or disappeared."

"Even if she didn't know *who* they were under there, Sarah's mother knew *where* they were. And if she did, so did my mother."

"And probably the whole town knew. Which might explain the thing about nets. The fear."

"Then we thought they could be the bodies of outsiders."

"What?" he broke in. "You think some people came down for a day at the beach, and the locals murdered them?"

"We talked about that."

"No," he said. "That's too stupid. They couldn't."

"Not unless they killed them one at a time."

He shook his head, refusing to believe. "They were all tangled up together, which probably means that they died together."

"So that doesn't make sense."

Sam looked from one to the other. "Well," he said. "I'm still waiting. So?"

"So then we wondered if they could be the bodies of locals, but before our time."

"Not too long before. The clothes are still there. So they're not that old."

"But locals not buried in the proper cemetery. Buried next to it."

"You see? Because they were not truly locals."

"More like outsiders."

"Like Aborigines."

"Your mother's people."

"Hannah's people."

"The ones who vanished."

He saw in their faces that they were sincere. They believed this. He looked away toward the lagoon.

"And were they murdered? All of them?"

"We don't know that. Not for sure."

Without looking back he said, "It couldn't happen. Not now. This is the twentieth century."

"This is New Canaan," Rachel reminded him.

"There might have been a fight. Those people get into fights."

He turned at once. It was Sarah who had spoken.

" 'Those people'?" he said. "What do you mean 'those people'?"

"Aboriginal people. How they live."

"How? You tell me."

"I don't mean anything. But maybe . . ."

"Maybe they caused trouble for the locals? The whites?"

"Yes."

They were suddenly quiet, afraid of what had passed.

"Sam . . ." Rachel said.

He did not answer. She tried again.

"Sam, Sarah got into the Father's place. Not the church, right into where he lives. She found a book. It could be that great book."

"Why not? We've got nets coming down out of the sky and signs and Fathers in white robes and Angels and fairy-tale gardens. Why not have a great book? What's it called? *More Tales of Fantasy?*"

"Would you believe if your mother's name was in it?"

He said nothing.

"You said she had the name Hannah from the beginning. It wasn't Hibbert who gave it to her."

"You said Hibbert called her Shadows, not Hannah."

"With a name like Hannah, if she came from here, we think the Father named her."

"And if he did, he would have named others. Even Aborigines. Like he named everything."

"So?"

"The Father and the Angel are at the men's service on the jetty. If you come down to the church now, I could show you the book and no one would ever know."

"What if her name is there? What would that prove?"

"It's not just her name. If the book is a register like we think, it could say how they died. It could have particulars."

He laughed. "You were in the church with me that day. He couldn't care less about her or the Aborigines. They might never have existed."

"But he lies, he always lies. They mightn't have vanished."

"Something else might have happened. Like we were saying."

"And our mothers knew."

"But old Gray Eye kept them quiet. Blackmailed everyone. Made them work for him."

"Worship him."

"And that explains the fear. Because it wasn't just one person who buried those bodies . . ."

"Because there's not just one killer . . ."

"But a whole town full." He had finished their sentence himself.

III

They followed Sam's track through the bush, the afternoon sun strong on their backs. Rachel and Sam walked ahead, talking, but Sarah came behind, full of her own thoughts.

At the entrance to the cemetery, she stopped and called, "Hey, you two, wait for me."

When she caught up, she said, "Dad and Joseph would have gone to the service. I should go home and check on my mother. She reckons those tremors were signs. She's expecting something—I don't know what, but she's waiting. I won't be long. I'll meet you at the church."

"Have you got time?" Sam asked.

"No," Rachel answered. "She hasn't. When that service is over, the Father will be back. Sarah, you go on with Sam. You know where the book is, I don't. I'll go check on your mum. I can cut through here to the tea-tree path, see if she's OK, then go on to the church. I'll run. It won't take long and they won't see me."

Before Sarah could agree, Rachel was gone.

IV

At the church door Sarah turned to Sam.

"All these years with his secrets," she said, "and the first time I came here to clean, he showed me how to get in."

She bent down and took a key from beneath the mat.

He grinned. "Why lock it anyway? A huff and a

puff would blow the place down."

But when the door swung open, he was silenced.

By the setting sun the fisherman was glorious, his robes dazzling white. The two women glowed in ruby and sapphire. Yet where the figures had fallen from the net and there was no glass, shafts of sunlight burst through, penetrating the church to strike Sam on his chest, his shoulders, his face. He was transfigured in gold.

Sarah came up beside him. "You were here in the morning," she said. "The sun was in the east, at the front. The colors were softer then. Not burning, like now."

"Sure," he said, "but it's more than that. See? There are pieces missing. The people in the net. They're gone."

"They fell out in the tremor. The whole place shook, and they fell."

"You saw?"

"So did the Father. He was showing me what to do, the cleaning jobs. When the tremor came, we were right here. The figures fell all around him, on the floor and the altar."

"Did you get them? Did you pick them up?"

She shook her head. "I didn't wait. I wanted to get home. But he was still here, on his knees, right where you are now. I left through that curtain. A door was open inside, and I saw the book, I'm certain. I couldn't see any more because . . ."

He had moved to the altar.

"Here," he said, calling her. "He put them here."

Reaching into a recess in the back of the altar stone, he gathered shards of china and pottery, holding them out for her to see.

"They're just bits of china."

"Like bones," he said. "Like the bones in that pit. So fine . . . and white."

"Put them back," she said. "Don't handle them. Put them back."

He knelt to replace the pieces, but as he stood, the shining brass of the icon caught his eye and he reached out to touch.

"Don't," she said. "Don't play with things."

He gripped the shank of the anchor and lifted it, turning the gray eye on himself.

"Sam, we haven't got time . . ."

As she spoke, he pressed his palm against the vicious nails radiating from the eye, testing their sharpness, and with a cry, pulled away, shaking his hand in the air and dropping the icon with a clang.

"Bloody ugly thing," he said. "It jabbed my cut finger."

She ignored his extended hand and drew aside the curtain. "The Father has cleaned up himself. This fell too."

The door behind was ajar, and she led him into the

library. Immediately he saw the globe, beautiful even in that gloom.

"Don't touch," she said. "I want to see this book and get out. It was here . . . There was a door . . . Here."

She fumbled with a doorknob, making small sounds of frustration, and his hand closed over hers to help.

"It's locked," he said. "Have you got this key?"

She shook her head. "Not for here. After the tremor this door was open."

He was applying pressure now, twisting the knob one way, then the other.

"Sam, leave it. I'll look another time. I'll come back."

Then it gave and they stumbled forward.

The room was small, no more than a cubicle, but not dim, since above them, set high in the wall, was a window to the sky, its pane so clear that they could have reached up and touched the blue. The walls were lined with shelves, and on these stood bottles and vials of every shape, their contents of every color. There were racks of pens and brushes and tools for working both wood and leather, and sheaves of parchment clamped in presses or stacked under weights. There were strips of bark and polished hide and mottled skin, and stones for grinding and stones for sharpening, and many objects the likes of which they had never seen and might only guess at the purpose of, but in the one cleared space beneath the window lay a great book, for all the world a Bible, yet dull gray, and closed, and she said, "I told you."

"Do you think?" he said.

"I'm certain."

"Take it out," he said. "It's too cramped in here. Take it out into the light."

She did not hesitate. She went into the room, picked up the book in both hands, and carried it through to the altar.

"Shift that," she said, indicating the icon. "This is heavy."

When he had done as she asked, she placed the book on the stone.

He reached out, eager to touch. "Leather," he said, and she felt it too, running her hand over the surface.

"Yes, sort of. But from a shark. The tanned skin of a shark."

Immediately he pulled away.

"And see." She took his wrist, lifting his hand to rub it flat across the surface as she had done.

"See how he has worked it. All over. Like a net."

He felt the pattern under his palm, and then, tilting it a little to catch the light, he saw at once that she was right; there was the webbing of a net, intricately embossed.

"This Father has gone to so much trouble," he said.

She shifted his hands and opened the book.

There appeared a frontispiece of the night sky,

embellished with stars, and in a marvel of illumination, the words:

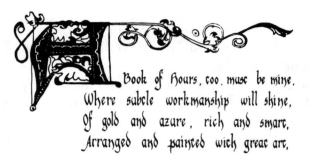

Book of Hours, too, must be mine,
Where subtle workmanship will shine,
Of gold and azure, rich and smart,
Arranged and painted with great art,

Filled with wonder, she turned the page.

Contained by a border lush with exotic vegetation, there now appeared the zigzagged backbone of a mountain range, and prominent among its peaks a solitary volcano sprouted stark and symmetrical arcs of red and orange and yellow, terminating in a sea of cobalt, so dense that it appeared to support rather than wash the shores of this awful place. And from the surface of the sea, creatures emerged: not the primordial lizards familiar to inhabitants of the Age of Science, but Monstrous Things—fanged and webbed—and some were head up and some were tail up, but none was quite correct there, since all seemed stuck in or glued onto that slab of blue.

"Dragons," he said.

"Chimera," she corrected.

The same scene was worked on the second page,

though this time the zigzagged range and the volcano were relegated to the edge of the far horizon, and no sea creatures were visible at all, but where they had been now flew or floated a white shape, dazzling against the blue.

"A gull," she said, but Sam whispered, "A sail," and she shrugged, turning to the next page, where the forest appeared to creep low as an animal lapping at the shores of an expanse of water which was, without doubt, the lagoon, since there was the bar and the headland and the core towering above, black against a red heaven. Here too was the same white shape fluttering over all.

"See," she said, digging him with her elbow. "A white bird."

But he dug her back. "Or a cloud. Or vapor, drifting off the surface of the rock. It could be anything."

On the next page was the lagoon again, but from its gray-green surround of bush, there now emerged another shape: not only the core but the spire of the church, and between the two a white form hovered, possibly winged, though indistinct, shrouded in clouds, and Sarah said softly to herself, *I think I see.*

Each page revealed another marvel. Figures appeared. Men and women, all workers. Here was the planting of the twin cypresses and there the garden and, later, the clearing of the bush and the construction of the paths and the jetties and the boatsheds and the houses. And in this landscape the people lived the cycle of their hours and days: there was net making and fishing and building and sewing and baking, and there were births and deaths and weddings and funerals, and the Father was in every place. No longer did he fly or float over land and sea in forms ephemeral, but as a man robed in white he walked the paths, naming and blessing, and without him there was nothing; no such country, neither man nor woman to inhabit it.

Sarah looked closer. She saw faces that she knew: Papa Rossellini in his prime, her mother as a girl, Rachel on the tea-tree path and with her the Angel, and then herself, in her own room, in her own chair, her bright hair flaming.

She saw the first of the signs, the sign of the hour-glass, and the second, the sign of the net—the tide-lapped Steele boys—and the third, the sign of fire, and the fourth—the sign of the serpent, its jeweled head rising from the sea. The next was unfinished, yet there was the Fisherman's Rest and the cypresses and two girls, one standing, one running, and a bike red and silver and a faceless figure, walking.

"Sam," she said, "it's us, me and Rachel and you, walking in . . ."

Rachel came up beside them, panting. "I'm here," she said.

"Did you see Mum?"

"She was standing at your gate, like she was waiting."

Then Rachel saw the book. "Is this it? Really? Is it?"

Sam laughed. "It's only a picture book. Useless. Old Gray Eye's fantasy land. A whole world of his own invention." Grabbing at the cover to close it, he caught the rough edge of a page and pulled away, hurt.

"Ow," he complained, "my finger . . . that cut."

Immediately the blood welled and a bright drop fell on the book beneath, on his own pale image, unfinished there, and it seemed that the picture changed; on the page before them Samuel Shadows appeared—fully fleshed, complete.

He stood speechless.

"It's just the light," Rachel said. "The movement of light."

"Sam . . ." Sarah began, but as she spoke, the first breath of night wind crept in through the open door, and the pages of the book fluttered and turned, and new images formed, merging and blending as shapes seen through water, and there was the core and there the headland and there the lagoon and the clearing, and figures formed, dark, naked, and some sat by fires ringed with stones, and some came and went between rough huts, and at the water's edge some waded among lush mangroves towing baskets of woven reeds.

"Oyster gatherers," Sam whispered, but hardly had

he spoken than the mangroves vanished, leaving only stumps, and among tin-roofed huts clothed figures came and went, their numbers fewer, their fires smaller, and the waters of the lagoon empty of life. And at this the light faded, and the shadow of a net was cast to signal night, and the Saturday lights of the Fisherman's Rest were dimmed, and there by the boatsheds were men the girls knew, and they named them as they passed, Rossellini first—since the net was his—then Buchanan, then Cataldi, and McCloud, and Slattery from the store—who was no fisherman— and their own fathers, no more than boys, and they were all drunk as lords, dragging the net down the tea-tree path, pushing and shoving, tripping and stumbling, and at the camp in the clearing, they fell quiet and spread the net wide, paying it out, loop by loop, unfolding it, until an arc was formed, and on a signal they advanced, cursing and swearing, hooting and laughing, until the black figures woke and ran, shrieking and crying, and far up the tea-tree path, the white wives cringed behind verandah screens, and the Father, alone at his table, looked up from his books and heard their cries, carried on the night wind, and smiled his faint smile, since the men would have their way, and had done since the beginning, and he sipped his tea while the net swept forward, dragging the black bodies, moaning and whimpering, over the edge, across the mud, into the channel, beneath the

dark water, and there, released at last, they drifted
lifeless to the bar.

"It's over," Rachel said, but still Sam looked since
there was the Father and his church was empty, and
there was no fisherman's window, nor altar, nor icon,
and at his door she appeared, a girl, hardly a woman,
dark and slender, and Sam knew her at once, his
finger touching, and as it did, there was blood, she
was bloodied and filthy, splattered with mud from the
mangroves, and she begged the White Father to follow, to show him what had been done in the night:
that her mother was drowned, her father was
drowned, her brothers, her cousins, her uncles, her
aunts; she begged the White Father to see what she
had seen by day: the bodies of her family lay in the
net, in the mud, the bodies of those that the White
Father had named, had baptized in the waters of the
lagoon, and he could see Amos and Abel and Eleazar
and Esther and Tamar and her baby, Ishmael, the last
he had named, and the White Father listened—since
she would not leave until he did, and there was nothing else to do in this church of pine where the pews
yawned empty—and then the White Father followed
her, his robe sweeping the sand of the tea-tree path,
and he waited, secret among the banksias, and
watched. And in the clearing where the mangroves
lay dead, he saw wives of the fishermen weeping as
they carted sheets of tin from the huts of the blacks,

and stones, dark and round, from the headland, and he saw fishermen dragging a net, new and strong, and from its webbing black limbs dangled and trailed, curiously supple even in death. And he watched as the net was dragged up the bank and across the clearing to the cemetery, to the seaward side, consecrated from the beginning by the White Father for his Black Brothers, and the net and its cargo were dumped into a pit, and the fishermen and their weeping wives covered it with the tin, then rocks, then sand so that none might see their sin, but the Father had seen all, and knew all, and stepped forward, smiling, and the people looked up, some in shame, some in guilt, but all in horror as the vision faded.

"Leave it," Sarah said. "We know. We have seen. Come away now. He will be back."

Sam shook his head, his face set. But when he looked again, there was nothing; the page was blank, the book lifeless.

"Show me," he shouted. "Show me who I am. Tell me!"

And in his own shadow appeared a dim room, and in it two persons, one, the girl, dark and slender, his mother, whom he knew by heart, and the other, the Father, touching her, stroking her, too close, too close . . .

"No," he cried. "No. That could never be." And he lifted the book and struck it on the altar, and the page flickered bright as fire, and there is the core, black against a red heaven, and as they watch, amazed, from its quarried face burst flame and lava, thick and molten, gouging the earth, cleansing it, and the waters of the lagoon steam and boil, and the church is filled with a great wind, hot as the breath of hell, and there is the Angel, crying, "Give me that book. Give me that . . ." and the book is slammed shut and snatched up, and the icon along with it, and the Angel runs from the church, leaving the altar stone bare.

Atonement

I

Sam braced his elbows on the altar and let his head fall forward onto his hands.

"He's gone mad," he said. "Mad. Everything's mad."

Rachel put her arm about his shoulders, pulling him toward her, saying nothing, but Sarah turned to stare up at the window.

"Look," she said. "Look up here. That's not the sun. Not that color."

The gaps in the leaden net were filled with a living light.

"Here," Rachel said, and when they looked, their skin, and the cold stone of the altar, were dappled crimson and gold.

"That's fire," Sam said. "There's a fire out there, I'm sure."

Together they ran the length of the aisle and burst out of the porch into the garden.

To the west the sky was red as blood. Black and mighty against it stood the core, its base wreathed in smoke.

"It's the same," Rachel said. "The same as we saw in the book."

"Not imagined," Sarah whispered.

Sam turned to them, lit from behind by the sky, the core at his shoulder.

"Then that book *is* true. My people are all dead, every one of them, buried in that net."

The girls said nothing.

"And if that's true, then the Father, he must be my father, mustn't he? I saw him with her, didn't I? When all the rest were gone, I saw her in his house. Didn't I? And him touching her. My mother. The Father touching my mother? In his house . . ."

They looked away, unable to face him. He buried his face in his hands, making no sound.

"Sam," Rachel said. "Leave it be."

He lifted his head. "Leave it be?" he said softly. "Leave it be? Sure. Like everyone here . . . for how many years? Twenty? More? Who knows? They were only blacks. Just a bunch of blacks."

He looked back toward the core, watching the sky and the smoke, and then, his eyes wide with sudden realization, he turned to Rachel. "The notes I made . . . the drawings. They're still up there, in the rocks. And my bike. We'll have to run."

"Run?" Sarah was appalled. "I can't run way up there."

They looked at her. "And what about this? It has to go back." She held up the key of the church.

"You fix it," Rachel said. "You put it back. We'll get the bike."

As they turned to go, she hesitated, adding, "And see about the Angel . . . why he took the book."

Then they were gone, crashing through the wilting garden, running side by side.

Sarah went back to the church. She sighed, Rachel's words sounding in her head: "You put it back. You fix it." She wondered, *Is that how it's going to be? Sam will leave now, and she is sure to follow. And I will be everybody's servant. My mother's, my father's, my brother's, and now his.* The door was open. The fisherman's robes were flecked with red. Rachel's words were very clear: "And see about the Angel."

"And why he took the book," Sarah repeated. "And the icon. And why he ran."

The heat was unbearable. The varnish on the door and the walls was crazed and peeling. She reached out, exposing the pale timber at a touch. *These walls,* she thought, *they're bending . . . warping.*

Suddenly, from the direction of the town, came a frightful roar. She turned to see, and there above the rooftops the cypresses burned as tongues of flame.

She looked down at the key in her hand.

"No," she said. "No, I won't put it back."

She ran down the path, flung the gate open, and was gone.

She did not stop, not even at her own house—until the jetties lay before her. In the failing light she strained her eyes to see. A net stretched wide over the Rossellini landing, but there was no movement. The boats had not gone out. The men would be here somewhere.

She went on, following the tea-tree path; at the boatsheds she heard distant voices, and breaking into a stumbling run, she came at last to the banksias. Above them, against the red sky, she saw white smoke billowing. The fire was closer here, moving toward the sea. *How?* she thought. *With the night wind rising, how can it move toward the sea?*

But when she stepped out into the clearing, she gasped in astonishment.

On the sand, among the twisted mangroves, all of New Canaan had gathered. There was Papa Rossellini with Slattery and his wife; Rachel's father, and with him the widow Steele; Joseph, her brother; and to one side, her father and her mother, standing alone and silent. She had never seen such a crowd, except at a funeral, and she wondered, *Are they here to watch the fire? Has someone died?* But before she could reach them, they began to move, walking together, taking the little-used path that entered the cemetery above the lantana.

Sarah ran as she had never done before—had never known she could—and dodging those at the back, she reached her parents.

"What is it?" she gasped, walking alongside, trying to keep up. "What's going on?"

"It's the core," her father answered. "They reckon it opened up."

"Opened up? What does that mean?"

"The quarry has split wide open. There's lava spewing . . ."

"I have been waiting," her mother broke in. "It is the last of the signs, from the earth, from the heart of the earth."

Sarah stopped. Her mother's voice was firm and clear.

"Mum," she said, "Mum . . ."

When her mother turned, her eyes bright, Sarah laughed.

"You knew, didn't you, all the time? But is it over? Is it?"

"Almost," Miriam answered, "I hope."

Reaching for Sarah's hand, she drew her close.

II

The people waited among the headstones, looking toward the core in silent expectation. It was almost night. About the base of the rock, the bush was burning fiercely, the flames lighting the sky with a savage glow. And suddenly, from between the stone plinths that marked the entrance, the Father appeared, and with him the Angel, both silhouetted against the light.

"What are they doing?" Sarah whispered.

Her father shook his head. "I wouldn't know."

Her mother answered, "He sent Angel for the book. And the icon. He's afraid."

Sarah moved forward, taking care among the headstones, until she reached the newer graves that lay unmarked and dared go no farther for fear of where she might tread. But now she could see.

The Father stood between the plinths, his robe billowing in the night wind, the book open in his hand; behind him stood the Angel, his chin high, his legs planted wide in defiance, the brass of the icon glinting in his raised hands.

As Sarah watched, first one patch of scrub, then another burst into flame until the bush between the core and the cemetery was a lake of fire, and from this, seething lava flowed, gouging the earth with white heat.

And the Father lifted his voice and cried out over the flames, "Return, I command, to your own place. None shall usurp my power. All is mine. All is mine."

He paused for effect—as had always been his way—and the Angel raised the icon higher.

They are *all mad*, Sarah thought.

But as the voice began again, the beam of a head-light swept the crowd and there was Sam on his bike, Rachel with him. The bike trembled before the entrance, between the Father and the fire, and Sam shouted into the stony face, "Get out! Go! You will die."

The Father cried louder, "All is mine, the earth is mine!" His words were swallowed up in the roaring of the fire.

Then Sarah ran to Rachel. Ignoring the Father and the Angel, they went among the people, driving them away, until all were clear of danger.

But the flow crept closer, and seeing this, Sam rode between the graves, calling, "Father, Father . . . I've come from the core . . . it's pouring out a river of fire. It cannot be stopped."

The lava flow had entered the gates, and as the people watched, the plinths tumbled inward, slowly and silently, and the bubbling ooze enveloped them.

Then the Father took a new stand. Among the old headstones he waited again, his Angel behind him, in blind belief holding steady that sightless eye. Sam pleaded, "Father, come away. Let what is past be over. Close the book. Destroy it. I am your son."

When they heard this, the people murmured.

And from the crowd stepped Miriam Goodwin, her drab blue dress made purple by the flames. Pointing toward the lava, she cried, "Read the signs now, Father of Liars. Know the power that strikes you down."

As she spoke, the flow divided, splitting like the tongue of a serpent, and the Angel, seeing clearly the flames that surrounded him, let out a great cry, and dropping the icon among the graves, he fell to his knees, hiding his eyes from the end that was to come.

From the safety of the new graves, Sam called once more, "Father, Father, if you have any love . . ."

The Father lifted his gaze from the book, his gray eyes cold and dead as ashes, and spread his arms, his robe as wings, fluttering white, then red, and the book fell among the flames.

At that moment the lantana roared, exploding in a column of fire, and there came a screaming such as none had ever heard, nor would hear again, and all was gone: the icon and the book and the Angel and the Father, and the lava flowed on to steam and cool in the dark waters of the lagoon.

III

In the morning Sarah stood behind the bright yellow barricades that cordoned off the clearing. *I could be in space,* she thought. *This could be the surface of the moon.*

Everywhere the masked and white-suited figures of seismologists and vulcanologists probed and measured. Once again all of New Canaan had come out to see: the wives from their verandahs, the fishermen from their boats, Papa Rossellini alone and silent, Mr. Burgess once more with the widow Steele, and Sarah—with her mother and father and brother—observing all, and talking among themselves as never before.

Later Rachel and Sam came down.

"We've been back to the core," he said. "I thought maybe we could get my things, but you can't get near the place. It's worse than this. There's scientists everywhere. The whole face is changed, isn't it, Rachel? All the quarry part, and the spring, that's where they say the lava came from, that pool and the caves, so . . ."

"So he lost everything," Rachel said, "except the bike."

"What was left of my camping gear, my tools for the dig, my instruments, my notes . . ."

"All your midden notes? For your paper?"

"What I got on Saturday is gone, but that was only the last of it. I have enough, back at the university. I can still do the paper . . . but look at this place now. The midden . . ."

"They say part of the cemetery has gone too. The old part, pushed into the lagoon. The lantana too."

"And what was in it."

"Over the bar by now."

"Out to sea."

"So they're gone. All my people."

"That's not true," Sarah said. "You're one of them. And you're here."

"Sure," he said. "Sure, the last of their tribe . . . their own black savior . . . resurrected white."

He laughed at his own joke and walked away to watch the scientists probing the sulphurous ash.

The white suits were dazzling in the morning sun.

As soon as she was certain that he could not hear, Sarah said, "When he goes home, back to the city, will you go too?"

Rachel nodded.

"When?"

"Late this afternoon."

There was silence.

"What about your father?"

Rachel pointed into the crowd. "Haven't you noticed? He's with Mrs. Steele. Some men don't take long."

Sarah had seen. "It makes leaving easier," she said, then added, "But what about money? I've still got that birthday money—that's yours, remember?"

"I remember," Rachel said. "I could use it now. Otherwise I've got nothing."

Sarah sighed, uncertain. There were questions she must ask.

"Will you stay with Sam?"

Rachel shook her head. "He boards at the university college. But he went up to the store this morning and called Hibbert. He asked her if I could stay at her place, and she said yes. So . . ."

"But . . ." Sarah could not finish.

Rachel turned then, her eyes brimming with tears. "Sarah, I love you more than anything. Anyone. But I have to go. Even though the trouble is over, I have to get out of here. I'll blow up if I don't, just like that mountain. You see, don't you?"

She hugged Sarah to her.

"Here," she said, taking the locket from her neck. "This was my mother's, until Dad gave it to me. You have it. Then I'll have to come back, to make sure that you're wearing it."

Sarah accepted, but when Rachel had fixed the clasp, Sarah said, "There were plans for the future, your independence. What about all that?"

Rachel laughed. "My future? What sort of a future did this place ever offer? But maybe now I could stay. We could go into the tourist industry. You could give tours of the church—once-around-the-globe sort of thing—until the place falls to bits and the garden finally dies. I could sell lumps of the core. Slattery is already counting on the souvenir trade. Then there's all these scientists . . . some of them look all right. Better than the Angel."

"You're being stupid now. What I said was sensible. You shouldn't . . ."

"No. *You* shouldn't. You worry too much. Listen. I'll get a job as a waitress or something, just temporary, to pay for my board. To get some clothes. Set me up. I want to go out with Sam. Not live with him. I want to walk down the street with him, you see, because I'm allowed, because it's OK. And when the new year starts, I'll study part-time. Sam's work on that midden was fantastic. He was outside, not all cooped up in an office. I'd like to study for something like that . . . and maybe, one day, we could be a team, him and me."

When Sam noticed them staring, he pointed. "Look, up there. That nest is still all right. The herons."

Now Sarah laughed. "I guess that's a sign," she said. "I give up."

So when the time came for farewells, it was not so bad. Rachel had only one bag, a soft canvas thing with a drawstring, and she slung it over her shoulder while they walked up the path to the church, still open, and past the store and the Fisherman's Rest until they came to the remains of the cypresses, where Sam was waiting with the bike.

"You coming too?" he asked Sarah, laughing. When she shook her head, he puckered up for a kiss, which she gave him, feeling the softness of his lips for the first time.

Rachel slipped the bag from her shoulder, hugged her, then sat behind Sam.

"No helmet," she said. "I might get arrested before I even . . ."

He hit the starter and the engine drowned her words, but she managed some sort of an awkward wave as the bike took off between the trees.

Sarah ran a few paces before she realized what she was doing—that she could run all she liked and she would never keep up with them, or catch them, nor would they come back now if she did—so she stopped herself and, feeling stupid, looked about to see if there was anyone watching. She walked back between the cypresses, charred skeletons now, into the town itself.

IV

That night Sarah sat with her family on the verandah. There was no fishing, and might not be for weeks, until the bar was cleared.

She said to her father and brother, "Instead of sitting there doing nothing, why don't you get up and take down those stupid screens? They're rusty and rotten, and I never knew what they were supposed to keep out anyway."

"Or in," her mother added.

"In the morning you might see right over the lagoon,

or up to the core . . . or even into the future."

She winked at her mother and went to her room.

Sarah closed her door gently and, turning on the light, stood before the cabinets that lined her walls. No longer were they empty. Every shelf was filled with books, their leather bindings and gold embossing catching the dim light of the single bulb. She trailed her fingers over the glimmering spines. *Wonderful books,* she thought, *bound in leather and trimmed in gold: books of the sea, of Antipodean lands, of the stars and planets and the firmament beyond; books of poetry and people. . . .*

She withdrew a volume. Opening the cover, she glanced at the flyleaf. *Ex Libris Liberty.* She said aloud, "Thank you, Sam Shadows, for your father's books."

She dropped into her chair, the book still open in her hand. But she could not read, not with the day that had been, and looking up to the window, she saw herself reflected there, the light crowning her hair in gold, the chair her throne, the bright rag rug her jeweled footstool.

"No," she giggled. "You're not the Virgin enthroned."

She opened the window to destroy the illusion.

But as she sat back, gazing up into the night, the book slipped from her hand. Reaching down to retrieve it, her fingers brushed another at her feet. She smiled and picked it up. It was the notebook from Rachel, plain, black, still untouched, and holding it to her, she whispered, "So, my little one, though you are not rich and smart, and I am no worker of great art, what wonders might I tell in you?"

Outside, from the dark and unseen sea, the chill night wind sighed and the dune sands, silvered by starlight, slithered and shifted. But beneath, Sarah knew, the earth breathed warm and strong, as it had done since the beginning.